ON THE TRAIL OF A KILLER?

"Which way, boy?" I asked confidently, but felt as though I might as well have flipped a coin. He hadn't been taught to track. I'd meant to do it someday. I'd been busy. I'd been lazy. Rowdy would choose a path for us, of course, but he might head us directly toward the backyard hutch of some family's pet rabbits or take us to the nearest bitch in season . . .

Praise for Susan Conant's
Dog Lover's Mysteries . . .

PAWS BEFORE DYING: "Superb . . . Beautifully written and plotted!" —Carolyn G. Hart, author of the prize-winning *Death on Demand* series

DEAD AND DOGGONE: *"Dead and Doggone* reminds me of my first dog . . . Sasha was a little dog, but she had a big, brave soul. She made me laugh, she taught me a lot, and she broke my heart. This book is like that. I'd award it Top Dog Honors!" —Nancy Pickard

A NEW LEASH ON DEATH: "Susan Conant deserves high praise . . . delightful characters . . . [an] enjoyable mystery!" —*Kate's Mystery Books Newsletter*

MORE MYSTERIES FROM THE
BERKLEY PUBLISHING GROUP . . .

SISTER FREVISSE MYSTERIES: Medieval mystery in the tradition of Ellis Peters . . .

by Margaret Frazer

PENNYFOOT HOTEL MYSTERIES: In Edwardian England, death takes a seaside holiday . . .

by Kate Kingsbury

GLYNIS TRYON MYSTERIES: The highly acclaimed series set in the early days of the women's rights movement . . . "Historically accurate and telling."—Sara Paretsky

by Miriam Grace Monfredo

MARK TWAIN MYSTERIES: "Adventurous . . . Replete with genuine tall tales from the great man himself."—*Mostly Murder*

by Peter J. Heck

MAGGIE MAGUIRE MYSTERIES: A thrilling new series . . .

by Kate Bryan

PAWS BEFORE DYING

SUSAN CONANT

BERKLEY PRIME CRIME, NEW YORK

This Berkley Prime Crime Book contains the complete text of the original edition.

PAWS BEFORE DYING

A Berkley Prime Crime Book / published by arrangement with the author

PRINTING HISTORY
Diamond edition / August 1991
Berkley Prime Crime edition / December 1993

The Penguin Putnam Inc. World Wide Web site address is http://www.penguinputnam.com

ISBN: 0-425-14430-5

Berkley Prime Crime Books are published by The Berkley Publishing Group, a division of Penguin Putnam Inc., 375 Hudson Street, New York, New York 10014. The name BERKLEY PRIME CRIME and the BERKLEY PRIME CRIME design are trademarks belonging to Penguin Putnam Inc.

PRINTED IN THE UNITED STATES OF AMERICA

10 9 8 7 6 5

To Vivian Carter Umbarger
in memory of
her coyote-dog hybrid,
Rowdy.

Acknowledgments

Many thanks to Joel Woolfson, D.V.M., and William Walker, D.V.M., for advice about this book as well as for their care of my beloved Alaskan malamutes, Frostfield Arctic Natasha, C.D., and Frostfield Firestar's Kobuk.

Author's Note

Several canine characters in the book are based on real dogs, including my own, but all actual institutions and locales are used fictionally.

Chapter 1

ACCORDING to family legend, allergies were the excuse my Aunt Cassie and her husband, Arthur, gave for failing to attend my parents' wedding. My mother, though, believed that the real reason they skipped it was fear: Arthur harbored an inborn terror of life itself, Marissa always argued. You might suppose that she referred to some aversion to the symbolic significance of nuptials, but she didn't. She meant that Arthur was afraid of dogs.

Arthur and Cassie's absence from my parents' wedding pictures, though, is somewhat less striking than is the presence in portrait after portrait of six or eight members of the bridal party, which, with the exception of my parents themselves, consisted entirely of golden retrievers. The highlight of the ceremony occurred as my mother marched down the aisle preceded by a flower girl who bore a basket of orange blossoms in her mouth and an usher whose task it was to thrust his muzzle into the basket and strew jawfuls of petals on his trainer's route to holy matrimony. Marissa, I believe, forgave her sister for forgoing the exchange of vows but not for missing the sight of that perfect brace in action.

The dogs' performance did not, however, pass unnoticed or unrewarded. After joining my parents in wedlock, the minister presented large white ribbons to the attendants. He had the authority to make the awards, of course; he was—and still is—ordained by the American Kennel Club as well as by the Episcopal church. My father, in fact, insists that Dr. Hooper performed the wedding itself in his capacity as an AKC obedience judge and that his affiliation with a secondary religious organization was incidental.

Cassie and Arthur sent nothing at all when I was born, probably because the birth announcement, designed by my sire and dam, took the form of a pink premium list for a golden retriever specialty show. Cassie probably thought that Marissa's mail had reached her by mistake, or else Arthur opened the envelope, succumbed to a dander-driven sneezing fit, and discarded the announcement unread. More likely, Cassie and Arthur simply failed to realize that the new puppy bitch was human. It's not their fault. My name is Holly Winter.

My aunt and her husband, then, can't be blamed for missing the point of my birth announcement, nor can my parents really be held responsible for their difficulty in deciphering my cousin Leah's, which we received when I was about sixteen. Unlike all previous birth announcements sent by Buck and Marissa's friends and family, this one was not headed: "Litterbox News" or "Something to Howl About." They were also puzzled about why the new owners had failed to specify Leah's breed. Marissa, though, rationalized her sister's slip: If the breed went without saying, Cassie's pup was assuredly a golden retriever.

Because of subsequent bad feeling between our families, as well as Arthur's allergies, I saw almost nothing of Leah during her puppyhood and do not know whether she enjoyed retrieving the special imported English hard-rubber, chew-proof balls sent by my mother together with a typewritten list of tips on house training. Even when Marissa died and Cassie was obviously grieved—and probably sorry she'd missed the wedding—Buck didn't forgive her or Arthur, because he still considered them poor sports and moral weaklings for having violated Section 24 of the AKC obedience regulations: "Dogs must compete."

In fact, before Leah moved in with me, I hadn't seen her for about ten years, not only because Buck stopped sending whelping announcements to her parents after my mother died but also because Leah's family had left Boston for a small college town in central Maine, and I'd meanwhile left Maine, gone to college, and moved to Cambridge. It must have been my grandmother who first told them that I live here. Although my editor includes a little biographical information with my column, something tells me that Arthur and Cassie don't subscribe to *Dog's Life* magazine and seldom even pick it up at the newsstand.

Partly because Cassie's voice sounds remarkably like Marissa's, especially over the phone, her rare calls always startle me.

My mother is often with me, but when she speaks in my ear,
I usually recognize the source as internal. Besides, I'm always
stunned to hear my mother's voice discussing any topic except
dogs, and Cassie usually drones on about people, including Arthur and Leah. One of the joys of dog ownership is liberation
from the boring self-centeredness to which Cassie's loveless
marriage has doomed her, or so said Marissa, to whom a loveless marriage was any union not blessed with canine progeny.

As my mother would wish, then, I pity Cassie and listen to
her blather on. I even phone her once in a while, and we exchange Christmas cards. Last year, for instance, my card
showed a breathtaking color photograph of Rowdy, one of my
two Alaskan malamutes, in his new red harness, pulling a sled
across the snow-covered lawn at Owls Head, where my father
still lives. Rowdy's big color-coordinated red tongue is hanging
out, he's smiling, and especially in harness, he doesn't really
look much like a wolf. Because of the snow, you can't see that
the lawn isn't a proper lawn anymore, and neither Buck nor his
wolf hybrids appear in the picture. In other words, I do my best
to introduce life and love into what my mother called Cassie's
blighted existence, which is probably why she felt free to phone
me one May evening to ask whether I would keep Leah for the
summer.

Arthur, it seemed, had obtained some frivolous grant that
would pay him to gallivant around Europe under the pretense
of conducting scholarly research, and although he had managed
to include Cassie as a boondoggling research assistant, Leah
couldn't go unless he paid her way. Cassie didn't phrase it quite
like that. She didn't have to.

"In any event," Cassie added in my mother's voice, "she
needs to study for her SATs." She paused. "Scholastic Aptitude
Tests."

"I know what SATs are," I said. "Believe it or not, I even
took them."

"And then there's Cambridge," Cassie said. "Of course, we
always hoped that Arthur would get the call, but . . ."

Don't be misled. Although Arthur went to graduate school
down the street from my house—at Harvard, in other words—
he didn't go to theological school. He and Cassie both think that
the entire institution is divine.

"But the trumpets never sounded," I said gracelessly, mostly because I realized that Cambridge was simply Arthur's idea of a classy-sounding boarding kennel. I wouldn't trust my dogs to someone I knew as slightly as Arthur and Cassie knew me. "How old is she?"

"Sixteen."

"And she didn't, uh, inherit . . . ?"

"She is in robust health," Cassie said. I took that to mean that she was fat. "And she *is* your niece."

"Cousin."

"But she does call you Aunt Holly. Because of the age difference?

"I'm not that much older than she is, you know. I'm only a little over thirty." And why would Leah have an occasion to call me anything? She hadn't seen me for ten years. My promotion to aunt was probably one of Arthur's transparent ploys to finagle two months of room and board. If Leah's species and breed had been what my mother originally supposed, I wouldn't have given in. Much as I adore golden retrievers, I'd have had to explain to Cassie that the first time her bitch tried to drink out of Kimi's or Rowdy's water bowl, one of my malamutes, probably my own bitch, Kimi, would crush her muzzle. But Leah wasn't, after all, a golden retriever, and I'm not Kimi. I said yes.

"So if you feel that way about these people, why didn't you tell her no?" Steve Delaney, Rowdy and Kimi's vet, has a quiet, reasonable voice. He is tall and lean, with curly brown hair and blue eyes that change to green. He'd arrived soon after I talked to Cassie and was sitting at my kitchen table fooling around with the dogs while I scrambled some eggs and toasted an English muffin for him. He doesn't really like breakfast for dinner, but I can't cook much else and hadn't been to the store recently, anyway. The alternative that night was IAMS Mini Chunks, which is more nutritious than my cooking and, in fact, may well taste better, too.

"Why? Probably because she sounds like my mother." By the time I was born, my mother had spent years obedience-training spirited dogs. A mere small person was no challenge. Don't think that she was harsh, though. She never raised her voice, but her tone made you want to do whatever she wanted. I lost her more than ten years ago, and, in case it isn't obvious already,

I'll tell you that I miss her all the time. "Also, I guess I felt sorry for this poor ugly, fat kid, with her parents taking off for Europe and obviously just wanting to get rid of her for the summer."

I buttered the muffin, scraped the eggs out of the two skillets onto the plate, plunked Steve's food in front of him, and let the pans cool so the dogs wouldn't burn their tongues. When Kimi first entered our household, I tried to keep track of whose turn it was to lick pans, but the concept of taking turns is somewhat abstract even for Alaskan malamutes, dogdom's geniuses—hence two pans. The concession stands at dog shows sell sweatshirts embellished with stylized paw prints and the words "My dogs walk all over me." I own one.

"I thought you hadn't seen her for ten years," Steve said.

"I haven't, but Cassie says she's robust, and that's got to be a euphemism, right? And the last time I saw her, she looked like Arthur, I think. Okay, guys. Here you go."

They didn't need to be told. Malamutes always know what's meant for them, and if it isn't, they try to convince you that it should be. Before the pans reached the floor, the dogs' red tongues were scouring them, and each dog's big dark brown eyes were scanning the other dog's booty to calculate the chance of finishing first and stealing what the other had left. All malamutes have brown eyes, of course, and the darker, the better. In case you didn't know, the blue-eyed sled dogs are Siberian huskies, although some Siberians have brown eyes. Malamutes, of course, are much bigger than Siberians, with strong bulky muzzles and rounded triangular ears set wide apart. At that time, Kimi, the bitch, weighed an ideal seventy-five pounds, and Rowdy was somewhere between eighty-five and ninety pounds, but don't go by weight. Malamutes have a thick undercoat of soft, short fur covered by a long outer coat of coarse guard hair, so they look bigger than they are, and they're even stronger than they look, bitches included.

"And," I added, "can you imagine? Here is a member of my own family—my mother's niece—who grew up without dogs. I mean, it's practically inconceivable. So obviously, she's kind of pathetic. She must sense this void in her life and not know what's supposed to fill it. So this idea crossed my mind that she could handle Kimi for me—you know, as a kind of therapy."

"For you?"

"She isn't driving me that crazy, and you have to admit, she's improved a lot. Haven't you, Kimi?"

Both dogs were sprawled on the floor with the pans clutched between their big snowshoe front paws. I'd painted the kitchen cream with terra-cotta trim when I had golden retrievers, but if I ever had the money, I intended to do it in silvery gray and white with a real slate floor, not more fake-tile linoleum. In the meantime, though, Rowdy and Kimi's wolf gray and white didn't clash, and, in any case, they'd have graced a hovel. Bonnie, who edits my column, won't let me say it in print, but Alaskan malamutes are the most beautiful dogs on earth.

When Kimi heard her name, she raised her eyes, but didn't release her grip on the pan. She growled softly.

"Her attention is much better," I added. "And, of course, I'll find a class for Leah to take her to. There's one in Newton, in some park. Rose Engleman called me about it the other day. I'll take Rowdy. She can take Kimi. It'll be a sort of emotional reeducation. As it is, she's probably terrified of dogs, and I'm sure she has no idea what to do with them. And mals aren't one-person dogs."

"It's generous of you," Steve said, as if generosity to my fellow human beings were as foreign to me as dogs were to Leah.

"So? What's that supposed to mean?"

"So it's nice of you. That's all."

Then we washed the dishes and went to bed. Doesn't *your* vet make house calls?

Chapter 2

On the day Leah arrived, the thermometer outside my kitchen window hit ninety, and the air was so saturated with moisture that the scribbled draft pages of my new column stuck together, the windows and mirrors clouded up, and my clean, odorless malamutes smelled like dogs. In the late afternoon, the pale gray cloud cover turned deep charcoal, and thunder began to roll. The downpour let loose just as Arthur's academically correct medium-blue Volvo station wagon pulled into the driveway at the back of my house, which is the barn-red wood-frame triple-decker on the corner of Appleton Street and Concord Avenue. The wagon was obviously a professor's car, five or six years old and dented, with a multihued collection of campus parking permits stuck on one of the rear windows. If Harvard had seen Arthur's car, he'd have heard the celestial brass, after all.

"Holly Winter?" It sounded like a genuine question, probably because he expected to find the yard filled with dog runs, the air rich with yelps, and a clone of one of my parents exuding dander in his direction. I'm not much like either one. Maybe that's too bad, maybe not. Marissa was spectacular, but Buck is a human moose.

"Arthur," I said.

I hadn't remembered how tall he was, and I'd forgotten his face because there was nothing memorable about it. He was wearing one of those complicated British intellectual trench coats with dozens of flaps, pockets, buttons, fasteners, and miniature epaulets, and his face, eyes, and hair were the same bland English beige. His head was disproportionately large and remarkably oval, his body long, thin, and straight. He looked quite a lot like a wooden spoon.

7

Leah did not, which is why her arrival is somewhat blurred in my memory. I remember inviting Arthur in, and I'm positive that he declined the invitation. If Kimi and Rowdy had escaped from my bedroom, where they were temporarily jailed to protect them from Arthur's hostility to their species, I'm sure I would recall the event. Arthur, I believe, stood in the rain yanking out Leah's gear and handing it to us, and we ferried it through the downpour and into my kitchen. We must both have said good-bye to him.

I clearly recall planting my wet feet on the muddy kitchen floor next to the pile of Leah's sodden belongings and staring at her. As a child, it seemed to me, she had had light hair, but as sometimes happens in golden retrievers, the color had deepened to a rich red, much deeper than mine. My eyes are brown like Buck's. Hers were blue. Her face was not oval like Arthur's, but triangular, and in envisioning her as ugly, I had been entirely wrong. And robust? She had what my grandmother used to call an hourglass figure. I haven't heard her use the phrase since Marissa died. The only glass object my own figure resembles is a test tube. Except for the shades of red in our hair that echo the blaze of Marissa's, Leah and I were nothing alike. I don't look like my mother. Leah did. The similarity was particularly amazing because it transcended the style of Leah's times. Her long, wavy hair was pulled into a lopsided topknot, and she wore a black tank top over a blue T-shirt over a white long-sleeved shirt above a pair of knee-length metallic blue and black shorts intended for the Tour de France.

"Is something wrong?" She sounded like Cassie, who, of course, sounds like Marissa, but her voice was higher pitched and less throaty than theirs.

"No, nothing. I'm glad to see you. I'm just . . . I want you to meet my dogs."

"Golden retrievers, right?"

"I used to have goldens," I said. "But I've had a conversion experience."

When I opened the bedroom door, somewhat over a hundred and sixty pounds of Alaskan malamute barged into the kitchen and ignored me. I have owned a lot of dogs, and not one has ever been allowed to jump on people, but I hadn't had Kimi very long, and before that, she'd had a laissez-faire puppyhood. Besides, anyone who knows anything will tell you that northern breeds are a challenge to train. Kimi wasn't trying to knock Leah over. Her aim was simply to get close to Leah's face, and since Leah didn't kneel down, Kimi rose up. Rowdy knew not to jump. He dropped to the floor at Leah's feet, rolled onto his back, and foolishly waved his great, powerful legs in the air.

"Wow! Huskies!" At least she sounded happy about it, and although I observed her carefully for signs of what my father believes to be satanic stigmata—watery red eyes, a dripping nose, blotches, and sneezing—I saw none. She rubbed Kimi's neck vigorously and looked down at Rowdy. "Is that one having some kind of fit?"

"No. And they're malamutes." If you own a malamute, so many people tell you what a beautiful husky you have that the response becomes automatic. I didn't mean to begin our relationship on a note of correction, especially because I was relieved to hear her say something that would never have passed through the speech center of my mother's brain. Marissa would even have known which strain of malamute they were: Kotzebue. "Alaskan malamutes. This is Rowdy," I said as I rubbed his belly, "and the bitch is Kimi. The female. The one with the black markings on her face. Rowdy, sit." He did. "Give your paw." Leah lowered Kimi, gravely waved her hand in front of Rowdy, and grasped his massive foot. He already knew the trick when I got him. I'd avoided teaching it to Kimi because pawing is dominance behavior, and no malamute needs instruction in bossing people around.

"Kimi, sit," Leah said. She made the same handshaking gesture that had prompted Rowdy. "Give your paw."

Kimi, who didn't know the routine, sat squarely in front of Leah, flattened her ears against her head in a display of dutiful submission, and gently raised a forepaw. She didn't squirm and didn't rake her claws on Leah's legs.

"Good for you," Leah told her. "What a good dog!"

The Julia Child of dog training was the late Barbara Woodhouse, a British woman whose TV series promoted the belief that dogs adore the sounds of d and t and that the correct way to praise a dog is to sing out: "What a good dog!" I was pretty sure that Leah had never heard of Barbara Woodhouse. Kimi kept staring up at her as if begging to be told what to do next.

"Kimi, okay," I said. That's the release word I always use, the word that tells my dogs that they're free to do what they want. Kimi didn't move. "Okay!" I repeated happily. Kimi didn't even look at me.

"Okay!" Leah said, and Kimi bounced into the air.

"Leah, have you ever trained a dog before?" I asked.

"You mean dog school?" The voice was my mother's, but not the tone of incredulity. Heftily degreed parents like Leah's should have instilled a proper respect for institutions of higher learning, but she sounded as if I'd asked whether she had an M.A. in découpage or a diploma from an accredited academy of miniature golf.

I let the subject drop and helped her to transfer the pile of possessions to the guest room. The house belongs to me, or will eventually, but I inhabit only the first floor and rent the second- and third-floor apartments. (In spite of the fresh Sheetrock, good floors, and new kitchens and baths in the apartments—and absent from my own place—I rent only to pet owners.) As I watched Leah haphazardly unpack, I realized that her luke-warm response to the prospect of obedience training stemmed from the sport's failure to require human participants to wear a uniform or costume. Collars are strictly regulated, of course—no tags, no pinch collars, and, obviously, nothing electronic—but handlers wear whatever they want.

As I lounged on the bed and the dogs nosed around, she pulled out footless dancers' tights, leotards, sweatshirts, football jerseys, running shorts, more bicycling gear, and shoes designed exclusively for marathons, walks, tennis, and aerobic workouts. I asked whether she danced, ran, walked, played tennis, or did aerobics, but she thought my questions were funny and admit-ted that she was not very athletic. She'd also brought a combina-tion radio and tape player that was three times the size of my television (and, as it turned out, ten times as loud), three or four hundred cassette tapes, the complete works of Jane Austen in hard cover, a stack of raise-your-SATs workbooks, and more cosmetics than I have cumulatively bought in my life.

"You're not really my niece, you know," I told her. "We're actually cousins."

She smiled, dashed over to me, and gave me a hug. "I'd rather have you for my aunt," she said.

Soon afterward, she asked a disconcerting question about a framed color photograph that hangs in my kitchen: "Is that your boyfriend?"

I thought she was kidding. "Of course not."

She looked blank.

"Come on," I said. "Do you really not know who that is?"

"No. Really, I don't. Is it some kind of secret?"

"Leah, that is Larry Bird."

Her forehead wrinkled a little, and she started to open her mouth.

"Larry Bird," I repeated. "The greatest basketball player in the history of the world." You usually have to discuss Bill Russell when you say something like that, but I didn't want to talk over her head.

That evening, as Leah was in the guest room simultaneously painting her nails and reading *Pride and Prejudice,* I called Rose Engleman, who was on the board of the Nonantum Dog Training Club, to double-check the schedule of summer classes. While I was getting the information, Leah made the mistake of patting the dogs. When she saw the fur embedded in the tacky lacquer, she yelled at them, booted them out of her room, and slammed the door. Twenty minutes later, she apologized to me and taught Rowdy and Kimi to lap her face when she smacked her lips and said, "Kiss!" It was the stupidest dog trick I'd ever seen, worse than "Say Your Prayers." Kimi and Rowdy thought it was grand.

Chapter 3

FAME was what sold Leah on Cambridge. The morning after she arrived, we did a tour of the Square and ended up at the sidewalk café that sprawls out from under celebrated Harvard's Holyoke Center toward the famous Out of Town News-Stand, across from the Yard and in walking distance of the Fogg Museum, the Longfellow House, and the Blacksmith House, but Leah was impervious to historical renown. She caught on to the propinquity of contemporary celebrity thanks to the dogs, whose presence in an eating establishment was illegal, but who'd been easy to smuggle into the outskirts and stash under one of the tables that are more on the sidewalk than actually in the café. Practically all my father remembers of his one trip to France is that dogs were allowed in restaurants, and according to an article in a recent issue of *Dog Fancy,* they're still welcome. To sneak a dog into an American café called Au Bon Pain is simply to add authenticity, as the proprietors must realize, even though the Cambridge (so-called) Health Department doesn't. Most dog diseases are species-specific, and there isn't a single one that a person can catch just by sitting in a café with a dog, whose mere proximity, of course, builds the human immune system so it can fight off the colds, flus, and strep throats spread by the legal customers. Have I digressed?

Because of our need to protect the francophile café management from knowingly violating the Cambridge restaurant code, we were perfectly positioned to person-watch and were doing just that when Leah spotted among the passersby a cigar-smoking man whom she recognized as the greatest playwright since Shakespeare, then five minutes later, a tall woman best known as the Barbara Woodhouse of French cooking.

"She's really famous!" Leah said in awe. "Everyone knows who she is! Do you think we could ask her to say something?"

"We'd have to follow her," I pointed out. "And what would we ask her to say?"

"Preferably," Leah said, "we could have her wish us *Bon appétit.* But anything would do. I could bump into her by accident. You know, just jostle her a little, not knock her over or anything."

"Good."

"And I'd say I was sorry, and then she'd have to say that it was perfectly all right or something. Or maybe Kimi would do something to her, and we'd have to apologize."

"Sure," I said. "All I do is sic my dog on Julia Child. Then we get to hear how she sounds in person. Leah, for one thing, for all I know, she is afraid of dogs."

"I'll bet she isn't, and if she is, we could at least hear her shriek," Leah said happily. "It would be better than nothing, wouldn't it?".

The same reverence for public renown that sold Leah on Cambridge soon blended with her sense of fairness to sell her on my dog-training plans as well. As soon as she heard that Rowdy had an obedience title, she started making a game of kowtowing to him and calling him Sir Wowee.

"His name is Rowdy," I said in defense of his dignity, "not Wowee. And his obedience title is C.D., Companion Dog. It's the first title. It's nothing special." Except for a malamute. In the preceding year, for instance, golden retrievers had earned 814 American Kennel Club C.D.'s, 370 C.D.X.'s, and 127 U.D.'s, and 20 goldens had become O.T.Ch.'s, Obedience Trial Champions. There were 26 Companion Dog malamutes, one Companion Dog Excellent, and not a single Utility Dog that year. Of course, there are more goldens than malamutes, but just ask yourself: Why are there more goldens?

"And what's Kimi's title? She's probably some kind of world champion."

"Rowdy is a champion in breed, too, but Kimi doesn't have a title in anything." Then I hammered in the point. "He does, but she doesn't."

What Leah persisted in calling dog school began a couple of days after my preventive rescue of Julia Child. "We'll eat a little

early so we'll have time to exercise the dogs before we leave,"
I said.

Leah objected: "They had a long walk this morning, and it's
hot out. They don't need any more exercise."

I had to explain that although I usually avoid jargon, I do
use "exercise," a highly technical canine obedience term, because I refuse to say that a dog has to go to the bathroom.
Rowdy finished his technical exercise before Kimi, who was
somewhere down the block with Leah, and as I was crating him
in the back of the Bronco, my next-door neighbor, Kevin Dennehy, ended his daily run by trotting up and dripping sweat that
hit the blacktop in loud splats. Even though Kevin holds a rela-
tively elevated rank—he's a homicide detective—he still looks
like a Cambridge cop. Six months earlier, when enough Nauti-
lus establishments had folded to convince Kevin that lifting was
unfashionable again, he took up free weights at the Y. The program he was following must have been designed to reshape his
body so it was too broad to fit through ordinary doorways unless
he turned sideways.

He asked how I was doing. When I said that I was doing fine
and heard that he was, too, he asked how my niece was doing
with the dogs.

"She isn't my niece," I said. "She's my cousin."

"So why's she call you aunt?"

"Because she feels like it," I said. "And she's doing fine with
the dogs. She isn't allergic, and they're crazy about her. They're
totally infatuated. I mean, the standard says that they're not
supposed to be one-man dogs, but this is ridiculous."

I expected some kind of response from Kevin, partly because
he's a friendly guy, but mostly because I knew he'd always had
a slight crush on me. He didn't reply at all. At opposite ends
of the lead, Kimi and Leah were bouncing up Appleton Street.
I'm not sure that Kevin even heard me. His glazed eyes were
fixed on Leah, who was wearing what looked like a heavily elas-
ticized black two-piece bathing suit over a yellow tank top and
a pair of shiny knee-length electric-blue shorts. Freed from the
topknot, her hair stood out from her head and curled down her
back like the coat of an unclipped apricot poodle.

"Hi, Kevin!" she said. "How's your mom?" She also asked
about three of his relatives who'd been visiting. In the couple
of days she'd been with me, I might add, she'd learned the

names of a few dozen neighbors who were only faces to me, and she'd ingratiated herself with Mrs. Dennehy, a strict vegetarian and teetotaler, who does smell hamburger and beer on Kevin's breath when he returns from my house, but only imagines that she smells perfume on his clothes.

"Hey, Leah, come on," I said. "We're late."

To make it to Newton by seven, I'd planned to leave at six-fifteen, and it was now close to six-thirty. Newton is Shaker Heights. Scarsdale. Maybe Shawnee Mission? The suburb of suburbs, it has big trees, bigger houses, good schools, and practically no crime. Stroll down a Newton street on any weekday, and you'll assume that it has no people except babies, their nannies, and the hundreds of work crews mowing the lawns and painting the houses of the invisible population. A national survey of places in which nothing ever happens once rated Newton the most boring community in America. Although it's only fifteen or twenty minutes by car from Cambridge, I always allow extra time: The boundary between the city and the suburbs is so steep that even my four-wheel-drive Bronco might not make the grade. Even so, Newton has lots of people who used to live here, because it's where politically minded pro-public-school Cambridge intellectual parents move when their kids are ready for first grade. The prospect of moving to Newton is the most powerful birth-control device in Cambridge.

But Newton does have parks, dogs, and the Nonantum Dog Training Club.

"I want you to know that this is not my regular club," I told Leah as we drove west along the river. "This one is much more competitive. Some of these people are obsessed with high scores—they really compete, even at fun matches, even in class—and I don't want it to get to you. First of all, they've got poodles and shelties and goldens, real obedience dogs, and you can't expect to compete with that. But more important, that's a sort of sick attitude. All you want to work for is getting Kimi in shape so she'll qualify sometime, right? Not necessarily this summer. Sometime. And the class you're in isn't for beginners. It's Novice for Show."

"Do you get grades every time?"

"At class? No. Never. Just at matches and trials. Hey, don't worry about it. Just have fun with her. That's what it's about." Remember, Holly? Scores don't matter. What matters is your dog, not your score. Say it often enough, and you'll shake that high-score sickness. Scores don't matter. "Scores don't matter, anyway," I said.

As I've mentioned, dog training is one sport that requires no special costume, but as Leah and I walked the dogs through the wide opening in the stone and concrete wall, past a tennis court, and into Eliot Park, she drew a few stares. I guess Pre-Raphaelite aerobic bicycling hadn't yet reached the suburbs.

Leah and Kimi and Rowdy and I were not, of course, in the same class. Leah and Kimi's Novice instructor was Bess Stein, who sometimes admitted to seventy-five, was rumored to be well over eighty, looked about twenty years younger than she was, and moved with the agility of a preteen. She was tall and angular, with salt-and-pepper hair swept into a loose bun plunk on the top of her head, and she had the one absolute requirement of an obedience instructor: a clear voice that carried well, even outdoors. Tony Doucette, who was teaching my advanced class, was a tidy little man with a pencil-thin moustache and hair-oiled waves who looked like what you'd expect if one of Al Capone's accountants had been deep-frozen in the thirties and then periodically defrosted to teach people to train dogs. I was always surprised that he didn't wear spats.

Our advanced class met near the tennis courts, which, I might add, had a crumbling, choppy red clay surface and lacked nets, probably because of a tax-cutting measure called Proposition 2 1/2. Bess's class gathered on the opposite side of the long, wide playing field granted to us by Newton Parks and Recreation. Beyond it stretched what looked to me, a country girl, like honest-to-God woods.

Novice obedience can get boring, but it has one giant advantage over advanced work: All you need is a dog and lead. While three or four of us were still hauling the high jump, the bar jump, and the broad-jump hurdles out of the van someone had driven into the park, Bess's group of about fifteen handler-dog teams was already heeling around. Leah wasn't hard to pick out, and I noticed two young guys heeling their dogs, a border collie and a German shepherd, very close to her. Steve Delaney would work his shepherd bitch, India, close to Kimi when India was almost perfect and he wanted to proof the exercise. All dogs deserve perfect scores in their own backyards, but to perform well at a trial, a dog has to ignore distractions: a kid with an ice-cream cone, the sudden blare of a loudspeaker, a burst of applause, or—the ultimate proof—an Alaskan malamute. But other handlers usually scrambled to avoid us. Even so, there they were, a burly blond kid with the sides of his head shaved clean, heeling a young male shepherd way too slowly just ahead of Kimi, and a younger kid, about Leah's age, with curly dark blond hair, whose black and white border collie was within inches of Kimi's tail.

When we finished setting up the jumps, sweaty work on that steamy night, Tony started running a handler and her black Lab through the Open routine, and Rowdy and I sat on the grass near Rose Engleman and her miniature poodle and a bunch of other people and dogs I knew from shows. The dog of Rose's I'd known best was Vera, a fantastic O.T.Ch. standard poodle—at least twice the size of Caprice, her new one—and always shaved, trimmed, and pom-pommed. Caprice was also black, but she was a miniature poodle with a close-to-natural Puppy clip and an impish expression to match it. That Puppy clip told me that Caprice was being shown exclusively in obedience. For the breed ring—conformation, looks, gait, not behavior—she'd have needed an elaborate, sculpted English Saddle or Continental clip. Smart, perceptive obedience poodles must realize that that shaved-hindquarters Continental clip leaves them half naked in public, and I always feel embarrassed on their behalf, but don't tell the poodle people that I said so.

I said hello to Rose, who was sitting in a folding chair with Caprice perched on her lap, and I made Rowdy quit sticking his snout in the poodle's face.

Rose had never been fat, but she'd lost weight since the days when she and Vera entered every trial within an eight-hour drive of Boston. I remembered seeing her once at a show when she'd had her feet propped up to reduce the swelling in her ankles. Kindergarten teachers have to stay on their feet all day, and I'd wondered how she managed to do that all week, then hit the road every weekend. She must have been in her mid-fifties then, maybe five years ago. The children probably loved her quiet, hypnotic voice as much as her dogs did. She'd probably never had to chase or yell.

"You aren't teaching anymore, are you? Did you tell me you retired?" I said.

"Two years ago, but not from dogs, of course." She stroked

Caprice's head. "I've used this place for years." She nodded toward the tennis courts. Courts are a great place to train because they're completely fenced in and at least somewhat suggestive of an obedience ring. The only problem with them is that they're usually wasted on ridiculous people who insist on batting a ball around when there's no dog to chase it. "I live around the corner. We're here every night."

"You look great," I said. She did, too. People who show a lot in the summer have good color, because the typical ring is located in the full sun in the middle of a field, and if you want to be in the ribbons, you have to train a dog under show conditions. Unfortunately, that also means getting out there in the rain, making sure that the dog doesn't break when thunder crashes, and downing him in puddles. (In case you don't train dogs, I should mention that that's *downing* him—making him lie down—not drowning him.) "Caprice looks terrific, too," I added.

A certain type of top obedience handler would then have recounted every detail of her dog's performance, complete with scores in all the trials in the past year. Not Rose. "This is a sweetie," she said as she patted Rowdy's big head. "And who's your friend handling the bitch? Your sister? Glorious hair." Her smile leapt at you suddenly, like a toy poodle finishing a recall by unexpectedly bounding into your arms.

"My cousin," I said. "She's easy to find in a crowd."

"A knockout," Rose said. "The boys must be beating her door down. Isn't that the cutest thing going on over there?"

I followed her glance and heard Bess Stein's voice ring out: "Let's have better spacing here. If the handler in front of you is too slow, just pass him. That's too slow for the shepherd, and if it happens again, get that malamute ahead of him. Halt." Bess was fairly free of breedist prejudice, but she talked like all other obedience instructors: "The shepherd," they say. "The Lab, the golden, the collie," but always, always, *"that* malamute."

As I watched the border collie almost sit on Kimi's tail and saw the handler lean toward Leah and say something, I finally got the point. It was a familiar one. Leah had recently proposed the same strategy when she wanted to let Kimi bump into Julia Child to create the opportunity to apologize. I quit looking, not because I can't deal with someone else getting attention when I'm not, but because the next handler Tony ran through the

Open routine was a rigidly upright silver-haired woman named Heather Ross with a silver Continental-clipped standard poodle called Panache who knew the exercises better than I did and was being drilled to score a perfect 200 instead of the measly 199 pluses he'd been getting for the past year. I'd watched him before, and every time, he'd wowed me.

"That's one of the top obedience dogs around, you know," a man said. "You know what . . ."

"We know," I said, hoping to cut him off before he accused Heather of bending the rules or complained that the judges always let her get away with correcting her dog in the ring. I caught his eye and shifted my glance to a skinny woman huddled in a lawn chair. "This is Heather's daughter," I said. "Co-owner, right?"

She smiled yes. She knew why I'd interrupted. She probably overheard jealous rumors all the time. Rose's turn came next, and I was glad to see her give Heather some competition. Although every nonbeatified obedience competitor envies the top handlers, some of the nasty rumors about Heather were well founded. Rose knew all the tricks, too, but she didn't use them all. Heather, I'm sure, savored Caprice's performance less than I did. She distracted me while I was trying to watch by telling everyone in mock-sympathetic tones that Rose had been in the hospital not all that long ago and had looked like hell for a while. I said that she looked wonderful and that I liked Caprice a lot. I did, but that's not the only reason I said so.

Somewhat later, after the best malamute in the class mouthed his dumbbell and anticipated the high jump, everyone commented on what a happy worker he was. Even the top handlers will offer tremendous support to someone with what's called a nontraditional obedience breed—and keep offering it until the second you become a threat.

Chapter 4

"Oh, *she* did fine," Leah said. "I'm all sweaty. I've never sweated so much in my life. So when does she get to go to a show? Hi, I'm Leah. I'm Holly's niece."

"Cousin. Rose, this is my cousin, Leah Whitcomb. Rose Engleman and Caprice."

Leah said the usual things with unusual sincerity and prevented Kimi from pummeling Caprice.

"Lincoln's having a match on Thursday, you know." Rose's bright blue eyes were on Leah. Training dogs doesn't keep your hair from turning gray—Rose had a mass of short white curls—but it does stop your eyes from fading. If your soul stays vivid, your irises do, too. "It's a fun match. Oh, you got the flier."

"Bess gave them to us," said Leah, holding out a piece of paper with one hand and reaching down to thump Kimi's shoulders with the other.

"Rose, this was Leah's first class. Ever. She belongs in a real beginners' class. She wouldn't—"

"Oh, yes, I would," Leah interrupted.

"And I have the perfect book for you," Rose told her. "You stop by my house on your way home, and I'll give it to you. It's called *Training Your Dog to Win Obedience Titles.*"

"Curt Morsell," I added.

"She already has it?" Rose's face was eager.

"No," I said. "I've read it, but I don't own it."

"So you know it's perfect for her."

"Rose," I said, "the dog in the book is a German shepherd."

"So?" Leah said.

"So it's a good book," I admitted. Without giving away the plot, I may reveal that the book follows Morsell's son as he

21

trains a shepherd all the way through Novice, Open, and Utility.
"But it might be kind of discouraging. With a malamute?"

Rose dismissed the idea. "It's the individual that counts."

My individuals who counted would have yelped at Caprice
if I'd let her ride in their car. I drove, and Leah kept Rose company while she walked Caprice home along the edge of the
wooded park to what turned out to be a prosperous-looking red
brick house. The roof was gray slate, the casements had tiny
diamond-shaped panes, and multicolored leaded-glass panels
flanked the entry. A yellow bug light glowed in a wrought-iron
cage over the front door, and a collection of artfully placed
floods illuminated a lawn-serviced landscape of weed-free grass,
pruned rhododendrons, and enough fir-bark mulch to smother
all the vegetation in a square mile of tropical rain forest.

I parked in front and lowered the windows to make sure Kimi
had enough air. Then I let Rowdy out of his crate, snapped on
his lead, and was trailing after him toward a fire hydrant when
a bunch of louts hanging around some cars in the driveway of
the next house started that raucous, hackneyed meowing routine usually pulled by gangs of young men threatened by the
sight of a slightly built woman with a big, macho dog. From
somewhere in back of the house, a dog began barking.

"Don't pay any attention to those awful things they're saying," I told Rowdy quietly. "They're just jealous."

A master of understated ritual display, he swaggered to the
fire hydrant and cocked a hind leg. If the dog doesn't react to
the human pussycats, they usually quit right away, but when
Leah and Rose appeared, this gang suddenly crossed species and
shifted to mynah bird whistles and baboon shrieks. Except to
quicken her pace, Leah ignored the show.

"I'm sorry. It's like living next to a reform school." Rose
smiled, but her jaw tightened. "Come in."

She kept apologizing as I put Rowdy back in his crate, locked
the car, and followed her inside.

"Rose, really, it's okay," I said. "It isn't the first time anyone's ever given Leah a hard time. She can handle it. I think
we were just surprised. You know, Newton?"

Rose corrected me. "Newton isn't the way people think. It's
much more diverse. People have a stereotype, the way they
think it's all Jewish. It isn't, you know. Thirty percent. And peo-

ple think it's a town, including people who live here, but the population is about ninety thousand. That's a city."

She led us into the kind of grown-up dining room you hardly ever see in Cambridge. The china cabinet was filled with Spode place settings and vegetable dishes instead of paperback books or Peruvian artifacts. An arrangement of yellow lilies and snapdragons replaced the usual stacks of academic journals and reprints on the long teak table. Arrayed on the sideboard were a couple of decanters topped with stoppers instead of transformed into makeshift Chianti-bottle candle holders, and neither Russian icons nor Zuni fetishes placed the menorah in a meaningful cultural context.

Rose's husband, Jack, a burly guy with radiant health-club skin, walked in from the kitchen carrying a plate that held a mound of potato salad and a fat, lettuce-garnished sandwich on a bulkie roll. When he was introduced to Leah, he didn't make her self-conscious by remarking on her beautiful red hair or, worse, asking where she'd got it. Although I don't think he'd ever owned a dog, I'd met him at shows. Once years ago when my old car broke down at a show in Rhode Island, he'd located a mechanic to patch it up and insisted that he and Rose follow me back to Cambridge in case it conked out again. Two weeks later, when the same thing happened at a show in Portland, Maine, my cousin Sarah, who lives there, lectured me about joining Triple A and directed me to a Holiday Inn.

"Thanks," I said when he offered us food, "but we've eaten."

"Just a little something," Rose said.

After Jack covered the table with plates of sandwiches and containers of potato salad, coleslaw, and pickled tomatoes that we had with iced tea, he joined Rose in apologizing for the louts next door, but also tried to temper her indignation.

"It was that Dale." Rose's pretty voice was angry. "I caught sight of him, all right. He's the one with all the hoodlum friends. Mitch is outgrowing it, and Willie's always just let himself get dragged in." Her clenched fist rested on the table, and Jack covered it with his hand.

"Enough," he told her, then, glancing at Leah, added, "The less said, the better."

Rose ignored him. "Willie is not a bad boy. You know, he was at dog training tonight? I was so surprised to see him. With the new dog? Obviously he's been reading a dog-training book and practicing on his own."

Willie, it seemed, had been one of Leah's two admirers in the Novice group, the one with the half-shaved head and the young, light-coated German shepherd.

"The dog is Righteous. I didn't get the guy's name." Leah already spoke like a true dog person.

"Willie's one of mine." Rose sounded as if a poodle of hers had whelped his litter.

"Rose was his kindergarten teacher," Jack translated for Leah. "Everyone here had Rose."

"Not everyone," Rose corrected him. "Newton has open enrollment. But quite a few. Case is a small school, only one kindergarten. You know where it is? Not far from the park. So I had most of the neighborhood children. Willie was mine. The other two started at Ward, but, if you ask me, the parents decided it was too Jewish, and they switched to Case, in spite of me."

"Then you've been neighbors for a while?" I said. "I mean, you've had to . . ."

Jack contemplated a forkful of coleslaw. "Fifteen years."

"And," Rose said, "they'll never move because Edna won't leave the house."

"Edna Johnson, the wife. She suffers from agoraphobia," Jack said sympathetically. "All the more reason to overlook what—"

Rose slapped an open palm on the table. "Overlook! Don't—"

"Rose, enough," he said firmly. "This is not—"

"You're right. I'm making it worse." She smiled at Leah. "And the truth is, they are not the only ones. The woods . . . You know that's still Eliot Park, across the street. Eliot Woods, they call it. Well, it's . . ."

"It's a lovers' lane," Jack finished.

"Lovers' lane!"

"It's only in the summer," Jack said. "They drink beer, they carouse. Who knows?"

"Who knows? I know. You know."

"Every town in the world, there's a lovers' lane," Jack said calmly and indulgently.

"The problem next door," Rose said, "is who would bring friends home there? With his drinking and her . . ."

Jack nodded to her. "So you see? Who could blame them? They throw beer bottles, cans. It's nothing," he explained to me. Then he turned to Rose. "So now we pick them up and recycle them. So what?"

We stayed for another hour or more. Jack almost succeeded in keeping Rose off the topic of the family next door. Her occasional returns to it left me with the vague impression that there had been years of trouble between the two households, including some trouble involving dogs. Mostly, though, Rose and Leah outlined a totally unrealistic program of taking Kimi to matches during July, then entering her in some trials in August. Fun matches, fine. They really don't count, and you can correct the dog in the ring. You can't at a sanctioned match, but they're practice, too. Trials are the ones that count. As Rose had to explain to Leah, obedience trials are usually held in conjunction with dog shows, especially in this part of the country, so obedience people usually just say they're going to a show. Really, though, a show is for competition in breed—in other words, looks, conformation (how well does each dog conform to the breed standard, the ideal?)—and a trial is for obedience.

"Are they ever nice!" Leah said in the car on the way home. "You know what? My mother is right, and my father is totally wrong."

"Well, he is allergic," I said.

"Not about dogs. About Jewish people."

"What does he say?"

"He says they're all right, and he's got nothing against them and everything, but that they make you feel excluded. I don't think that's true at all."

"There are members of our own family who've made me feel more excluded than Rose and Jack do. Take Sarah, for example. You know Sarah, right?"

"Yes."

"Well, one time I was at a show in Portland, and my car broke down—this was in the middle of winter—and you know what Sarah did?"

"Sent you to a Holiday Inn."

We both laughed.

"How did you know that?" I asked.

"She did it to me once, too. My mother asked if I could stay for one night, and she said there wasn't any room and I should go to the Holiday Inn. And her house has eighteen rooms."

"And when Chrissie got married, I'll bet she didn't invite you to the wedding, did she?"

"No," Leah said. "My mother said she was afraid she'd have to feed us."

"You didn't miss much. It was those tuna fish sandwiches on Wonder bread."

"With the crusts cut off," Leah said.

"That's why people make jokes about Protestant weddings," I said.

"My father says that it isn't being stingy. It's just avoiding conspicuous consumption."

"Well, at Chrissie's wedding, anything to consume was so inconspicuous you could've starved to death. And she didn't even invite you. Talk about people who make you feel excluded. I mean, these are people who don't just make you *feel* excluded. They actually leave you out."

Chapter 5

"UGLY," pronounced Kevin Dennehy, who had planted himself squarely on one of my kitchen chairs with his feet apart on the floor. His thighs are so massive that if he sits down with his feet together, he has to spread his knees like a frog in mid-kick. His arms were crossed on his chest, and the muscles in his cheeks and jaws looked as if he'd figured out how to bulk up his face with free weights. He repeated the word and glowered: "Ugly."

"It is ugly," I said. "Didn't something like this happen a while ago in Weston?"

"Yeah. And in Newton before, too. One of the high schools." He was talking to me, not to Leah.

"So what did it say exactly?" she asked him. Dressed in hot-pink running shorts over a black leotard and footless tights, she was perched on a stool drinking a glass of a diet drink called Crystal Light, the one food—if you can call it that—she'd asked me to buy for her. It tasted so impotable that even Kimi refused to steal it. "When they called, they just asked if I'd seen anything. They didn't say much."

"Swastikas," Kevin said. "And anti-, uh, Semitic words. Spray-painted. In red." His eyes rested briefly on Leah as if she might not understand the symbolism of a swastika, the meaning of *anti-Semitic,* or the significance of the color red.

"All of that is fascist, you know," she informed us. "It's from Nazi Germany, including the color."

"Actually, we do know." I tried to sound as if Kevin and I happened to be unusually well informed.

The graffiti had been discovered early that morning by a runner taking a shortcut through Eliot Park. He called the police, who talked to the neighbors and discovered either from them

27

or from Parks and Recreation that Nonantum had been using
the park the previous night. The Newton police had called me
and everyone else from the club to ask if we'd noticed anything.
Leah and I hadn't seen anything to make us suspicious. The
Newton police hadn't told us any details of the incident, and
Kevin knew the few he did only because John Saporski, his col-
league and buddy, grew up in Newton.

"So," I went on, "all we know is that it happened sometime
after we left and before this jogger ran through there, so sometime in the night. Did any of the neighbors see anything?"

"Not unless they got X-ray vision." Kevin shifted in his seat.

"The wall. Right." I nodded. That's where the graffiti were
painted, on the inside of the concrete and stone wall that sur-
rounds the park entrance. I'd assumed it was a WPA project.
It had that carefully designed, perfectly constructed, labor-
intensive look. "Anyway, someone could've noticed someone
going in or coming out. Or maybe a car was parked there or
something."

"Could be," said Kevin unenthusiastically.

"Maybe someone will remember something, someone who
isn't home from work, someone they haven't talked to yet."

"Maybe," said Kevin.

Steve and I finally got some time alone that evening because
Leah had a date to go into Harvard Square with a kid she'd met
at dog training. His name was Jeff Cohen. He was tall and gan-
gly, with curly dark blond hair destined to turn brown by the
time he reached eighteen, and he turned out to be the handler
of the snazzy black and white border collie I'd noticed in Bess's
class. Unfortunately, he didn't bring the dog when he came to
pick up Leah, but otherwise, he seemed pleasant and trustwor-
thy enough. He shook hands with Steve and me, admired the
picture of Larry Bird, and apologized to my disappointed dogs
for leaving them home. Steve and I decided that there can't be
too much wrong with a Celtics fan who owns a border collie.
Border collies are smaller than rough-coated collies like Lassie.
I can't write it in *Dog's Life* or say it aloud in my own house,
but the border collie is undoubtedly the most intelligent and
trainable breed in the world. Trained border collies understand
seventy or eighty commands and control flocks of sheep by star-

ing at them with their eerie, hypnotic eyes. Owning one is a sign
of good character. And he brought Leah home at exactly eleven.

The next time I saw Jeff Cohen was on Thursday evening.
He and his dog, Lance, were warming up for the ring in a grassy
area by the parking lot of the Lincoln Kennels. The town of Lincoln is a rural suburb with lots of high-tech industry executives
who build discreet glass and wood palaces in the forest, join the
Audubon Society, buy Labs and golden retrievers, and have
them trained and boarded at pretty, pastoral Lincoln Kennels.
Jeff's dog looked at home in the country setting, and in spite
of the muggy heat that would make most of the dogs lag, this
one was keeping his strange, piercing eyes fixed on Jeff, who held
himself rigid.

"Jeff looks a little nervous," I said to Leah as I killed the engine.

"He'll be all right," she said. "Let's go."

"We have to exercise them first," I said. "Soiling in the ring
is an automatic disqualification. Then we check in. Then we
warm them up. Just a little heeling, sits, a couple of finishes.
Nothing that even looks like real training."

I'd insisted on grooming and bathing the dogs. A lot of people
don't bother just for a fun match, but Marissa always maintained that turning up with a grungy dog tells the judge, the
dog, and everyone else that you have no respect for the sport.
For an indoor trial, I always dress up, and for an outdoor fun
match like this one, I wear new jeans and a decent-looking shirt.
Leah had French-braided her hair into an elaborate series of de-
mure plaits and exchanged her multi-exercise outfits for a pair
of jeans and a plain blue T-shirt she'd borrowed from me.

Ten minutes later, when we'd registered and fastened on our
armbands, we spotted Rose Engleman sitting in a folding chair
near the Utility ring, which, like the other rings, was simply a
roped-off rectangle in the middle of the field. Perched in Rose's
lap, Caprice was evidently assessing the competition. A couple
of other people with real obedience dogs—a sheltie and a golden—were talking with her. Heather and Abbey, though, had
set up their chairs so close to the ring entrance that they were
all but in it. Between their chairs was a silvery gray polypropyl-
ene crate. A thermos and two cups sat on top of it. I assumed
that Panache, Heather's poodle, was inside.

We'd have settled down near Rose, but it is against my princi-

ples to station a malamute anywhere near an obedience ring.
No matter how perfectly the malamute behaves, something
about the scent or appearance of the breed constitutes an unfair distraction to the dog who's working. We did say hello to
her, though, and then, with only about ten minutes until our
turns, we found an unoccupied place on the little hill above the
rings, where we spread out a blanket, gave the dogs some water,
and dampened their bellies to help them cool off.

"If it starts raining, she's going to break on the down," I told
Leah, who really belonged in Pre-Novice where Kimi would
never have been off lead. In case you don't train dogs—really?
why not?—maybe I should add that on the down, the dog is
supposed to hit the ground and stay there. Standing up or moving around instead of staying is optimistically known as breaking, but, in truth, I hoped that Kimi didn't shatter to pieces by
leaping out of the ring or pouncing on another dog. Kimi belonged in Pre-Novice, too, but Leah had spurned my advice.
And want to hear something unfair? Since Kimi was registered
to me and I'd put titles on Vinnie, Rowdy, and lots of other
dogs, my experience forced Leah into Novice B, even though
Leah herself had never owned any dog or entered any match
or trial before. In fact, if I'd done nothing more than put a C.D.
on Rowdy, Leah would still have had to enter B instead of A.
Most of the handlers in Novice B aren't novices at all. "She
hates wet grass," I added, "so don't be disappointed. And in
this heat, she's going to lag. When she does, give her an extra
command. Just say, 'Heel.' You'll lose points, but you can still
qualify. All she has to do is stay within six feet of you. And
whatever you do, don't slow down yourself. If the judge thinks
you're adapting your pace, you'll lose a lot of points."

"I know, I know," she said, but smiled tolerantly. "You already told me. Relax, would you? It's a fun match. Fun, right?"
She stroked Kimi's face and ran her fingers over the black of
her Lone Ranger goggles.

"Fun," I said. "Okay. All you do now is wait near the entrance to your ring. Keep her sitting at heel, and keep her attention on you. The stewards will tell you when it's your turn."

As Rowdy and I waited at ringside—we were in Open—I saw
her enter the Novice B ring, and I noticed how composed she
looked and how straight Kimi sat as the judge spoke to Leah.
After that, my attention was on my own judge and on Rowdy,

who slowed down in anticipation on the Drop command, but hit the ground smartly when it came and otherwise did pretty well. When we left the ring, Leah and Kimi were already on our blanket, and Kimi was chewing up the last bits of a dog biscuit. That didn't mean a thing. I'd instructed Leah to reward Kimi no matter what happened.

"So how was it?" I asked.

"Great!" The normal response from a first-time handler at a match consists of a detailed account of everything that went wrong and concludes with a vow never to enter a ring again, at least with this dog. "The judge was *so* nice."

"Did he say you qualified? So far?" In case you don't show in obedience, I should say that after the Novice and Open individual exercises—the ones in which you and your dog are the only team in the ring—come the group exercises, the long sit and the long down.

Leah's face fell.

"If you hadn't, he'd probably have told you." Some of the judges at fun matches aren't yet American Kennel Club judges—they do fun matches for experience—and they occasionally forget things. I questioned Leah about the obvious errors that would have made Kimi fail—not coming on the recall, leaving the ring, soiling, walking away on the stand for examination—and Leah claimed that Kimi hadn't committed any of them. "So you probably qualified. That's fantastic. Congratulations. We've qualified, too. So far."

The time between qualifying in the individual exercises and reentering the ring for the sits and downs is nerve-racking for most beginners. Leah drank some water from the dogs' thermos, stretched out on the blanket between them, and propped herself up on her elbows to watch Jeff and the border collie, who were in the Pre-Novice ring. Rowdy was nuzzling the blanket in search of stray crumbs from his giant-size Old Mother Hubbard biscuit, Kimi was resting her lovely head on her forepaws, dogs and handlers were working in all the rings, Leah's eyes were heavy, and the long day of heat and humidity was drugging me. I felt illuminated: the hot, damp greenery, my unexpected cousin, my beautiful dogs, other dogs, other handlers, a momentary satori in canine Zen. Then it broke.

"You want to see something?" I said to Leah. "Watch over there, the Utility ring. You see the silver standard poodle?"

"He was there the other night."

"That's the one. And opposite is Heather, his handler, right? With the silver hair?"

"So?"

"So look in back of Heather, outside the ring. You see that really skinny woman with long brown hair? In the green flowered shirt?"

"Yeah."

"Notice that her arms are crossed. Her hands are closed, sort of in fists, as if she's got something in them. And she's watching the dog, right? That's called double handling. That's Heather's daughter, Abbey, and they've practiced this routine so they've got it cold. It's illegal to take food into the ring, but the dog's been taught there's something in Abbey's hand, liver or something, and Abbey stations herself where the dog can see her. If the dog starts to break, she probably moves her hand a little, or does something, something really subtle."

"That's cheating!"

"It's a mother and daughter act," I said.

The silver poodle didn't break, of course. I watched until the end. Then I heard a deep male voice hollering.

At the edge of the field closest to the parking lot, Rose's ex-student, Willie, was leaning on the long registration table. He seemed to be filling out an entry form. He looked as if he might be trying to bury his face in it. His blond German shepherd lay on the ground at his feet. About five yards beyond the end of the table, another blond young man was shouting at another shepherd, a cowering, snarling dog that kept lunging toward him.

"Kaiser, you bastard, down!" he yelled, and he yanked hard on the dog's collar.

"Is he supposed to be doing that?" Leah sat up. "Oh, God. You know who that is? And that's Righteous and what's his name. Willie. That's his brother. The one—"

"Next door to Rose and Jack. Yeah. And no. He isn't supposed to be doing that. Someone will speak to him. What are they doing here, anyway?"

"Bess gave us the fliers, remember? But you said—"

"I did, and it's not allowed."

Even from a distance I could see that the brother's shepherd had a long, soft, silky coat—undesirable in the breed—that needed a shampoo. If the dog had been scrubbed, I guessed, his pale fur would have looked washed out, not rich like the first dog's. When his handler took a step ahead, the dog suddenly jerked his head toward the man. It looked to me as if he tried to bite him. The man retaliated. He raised an arm and smashed the dog hard on the flank, and the dog yelped. In his unceasing hope that a fabulous dog fight would break out and that he could launch himself in the center of it, Rowdy leapt up, and Kimi, the radical feminist, joined him. If I'd stayed on the blanket, Rowdy could easily have hauled me across the field and into the shepherd's jaws, but I stood up, got a good grip on his lead, braced myself, and told him to sit. He did. Without being asked, Leah took charge of Kimi. In fact, she seemed so capable of managing the dogs that I started to hand her Rowdy's lead— I intended to step in, but not with Rowdy—when I saw that one of the judges, a man I didn't know, was finally going to intervene.

"There's a judge," I told Leah. "And somebody else. That is totally forbidden. You aren't allowed to do anything more than a little warm-up. You can't even really train, and hitting a dog is totally against the rules. At a show, they'd make him leave the grounds. I don't know what they'll do here."

The judges and the officials running the match were slow to respond, because, I suppose, they were as surprised as I was. Once in a while, someone who hasn't bothered to read the rule book starts training at a show or talks a little loudly to a dog, and dogs occasionally get aggressive, but most shows, trials, and matches are harmonious. The human participants who worship dogs, and the few who train harshly do so only in private, partly because they know the rules and partly because they want to avoid creating a bad public impression of the sport.

"That's *my* judge," Leah said proudly. "What's he saying?"

"He's probably telling him to leave."

By then, the shepherd, beaten into submission, was lying quietly by his owner. The judge was obviously lecturing. One of the people from the Lincoln Kennels, a guy who has shelties, was standing nearby with his arms folded over his chest.

Suddenly the blond handler hauled on the dog's lead, dragged the poor shepherd to his feet, and shouted at the judge so that everyone heard: "Well, screw you! You hear that? Screw all of you!" Heading for the parking lot, he added, "Come on, Willie. Let's get the hell out of here."

"Poor Willie," Leah said. "How totally embarrassing."

"Jesus," I said. "The poor dog. And the poor judge. You know, things like this don't happen. This is not what it's like."

"I saw a bumper sticker on a car the other day," Leah said. "It said: 'Shit happens.' I couldn't figure out what it meant. I guess this is what it meant." She looked at me and smiled.

She had that special gift of making things all right again. One of her other gifts was King Solomon's ring, the one that let him talk with animals. She and Kimi ended up with an impressive 192 1/2 (out of that perfect 200) and a second-place ribbon. Rowdy, who lost points for slowing down before the drop and for some sloppy sits, got a 187 and third place. Four ribbons— two for qualifying, two for placing—is pretty spectacular if the two dogs are Alaskan malamutes and it's one handler's first time in the ring.

The standard color for a first-place ribbon at a trial is blue, but at a match, it's rose. I'd missed the Utility awards, but on the way out, we ran into the suitably named Rose Engleman, who had her first-place ribbon in one hand and Caprice's thin blue lead in the other. Caprice was bouncing around and showing off.

"Congratulations," I said to both of them. Then I got down to business. "How did Heather do?"

"Second," Rose said. "By one point." Handlers like Rose and Heather, I might add, often enter fun matches noncompetitively. That night, though, each had clearly decided that the other's presence justified her own competition. Even so, Rose did not brag about her own score. She didn't even tell me what it was.

I like to remember her exactly as she was in those few minutes on that sultry night, a first-place ribbon in one hand, her dog's lead in the other, listening with the enthusiasm of an ardent newcomer as Leah went on and on about things that Rose must have heard a thousand times. She'd heard them all before, but she never heard them again. The next evening, as I learned later, she took Caprice to the abandoned tennis court at Eliot Park. As they were training, the heat and humidity that had been building over the past few days finally broke in another of the violent electric storms and downpours we'd been having all summer. Rose was prepared for the rain, I heard. She had on a set of those waterproof pants and jackets you usually see on runners about a third her age. Jack gave her the outfit for Christmas, he told me later. He picked out the color to match her eyes: electric blue. Maybe he'd had a premonition. Lightning strikes farmers. It hits people who are swimming or fishing or playing golf. I'd never heard of it killing anyone who was out training a dog, but ordinary handlers quit when rain starts. Top handlers train for all weather conditions and all distractions. If the Flood itself had let loose and God had boomed out a Commandment, Caprice would have been prepared. Maybe Caprice was. It was Rose who reached out and touched the metal door of the all-metal chain link fence.

Chapter 6

THE human denizens of dogdom are America's last true villagers. Every kennel club is a tiny town with strong home-group loyalties and a complex network of bonds with its neighbors: ties of history, rivalry, and divided allegiance. Like villagers flooding a market town, we gather *en masse* at dog shows, not only to transact our practical business but to renew our sense of oneness with our fellow citizens of the great and noble Republic of the American Kennel Club.

Bess Stein, Leah's Novice instructor at the AKC-member Nonantum Dog Training Club, had been judging lately at States Kennel Club and Continental Dog Association trials as well as teaching at two clubs on the south shore. During World War II, she worked with my own Cambridge Dog Training Club in the Dogs for Defense program that recruited and trained canine soldiers, and more than a decade afterward, she bought a golden retriever from my mother. All this is to say that it was Bess who called me on Saturday afternoon with the news of Rose Engleman's death by lightning.

I heard the phone ring only because I'd come inside to refill my glass with real lemonade and Leah's with fake. In the arid ninety degrees, Leah and I were playing Tom Sawyer with the section of fence that encloses the Appleton Street and driveway corner of my yard. We wore old T-shirts and jeans of mine—big on me, small on her—that had descended even below my relaxed standards for kennel clothes. Daubs of white Benjamin Moore augmented the bright freckles on Leah's arms and nose and the paler ones on mine.

I'm awkwardly blunt at breaking bad news, and espe
because Leah had seemed so self-confident and almost ne

like a human malamute, I was unprepared for her sobbing. When I'd jammed the lid on the paint can and dropped the brushes in a bucket of water, I put my arm around her shoulders, and I could feel her shaking. We sat in the shade on the paint-spattered grass.

"I shouldn't have told you so . . . ," I started to say. "Bess just called."

"Did it hurt her a lot?" Leah was crying so hard that I had trouble making out the words. I found her suddenly a child and myself suddenly the grown-up.

"I don't think so. It must've been almost instant. I don't know if it hurt. But if it did, it was only for a second. She was in the tennis court, at the park, where we had class the other night. This was last night, just before dark, when we had all the thunder. Remember?"

She nodded.

"It must've happened just when she was leaving. The lightning must have hit just when she was opening the door." The door, of course, was metal. So was the entire high chain link fence surrounding the tennis court. Did the metal burn? Did it hurt? I wanted a real grown-up to assure me that it hadn't. "Jack found her."

"What about Caprice?"

"She came home alone. That's how Jack knew something was wrong, because Caprice came home without Rose. He heard her scratching at the door. He went to look and he found Rose."

"Holly?"

"Yes."

"Could we not paint anymore now?"

A few minutes earlier, we'd both been Tom Sawyer. Now I was Aunt Polly, a character, I might add, I'd never liked: the enemy, the ultimate adult. Death means that someone has to be the grown-up, the person who gets stuck pretending to know what the hell is going on. When it comes to dogs, of course, I do know what the hell is going on, at least most of the time, and I don't mind explaining it to them and telling them what we're going to do about it and why. But when it comes to people? If Leah hadn't been crying and asking questions, if she hadn't been there at all, I'd probably have thrown a clean pair of jeans, a toothbrush, and my dogs into the car and driven to Owls Head, Maine, where Rose's death would have been far

away and where no one—certainly not my father—would have
expected me to pay attention to the needs of human beings. I'd
have written Jack a letter, sent a donation to a good cause, and,
when some time had passed, I'd have talked with people about
what a great handler Rose was.

One of the advantages of living alone—not that anyone with
two malamutes is really alone—is never having to explain why
you have to leave town. You put the dogs in the car and go.
There is no one—a cousin, for instance—who might assume
that you're running away. My mother disapproved of running
away. Every time one of our dogs died—and with a lot of dogs,
you have a lot of deaths—she made me watch everything, including the burials, especially the burials, because I was supposed to say good-bye and understand it was for keeps. The last
one I watched was her own. I haven't been to a funeral since
then. They all feel like hers.

We did not, of course, have to paint anymore. We washed
the paint off our hands and sat glumly in the kitchen drinking
tea, patting the dogs, and talking about Rose. To mourn Rose,
we still wore our ragged old jeans and shirts, as if we'd torn our
clothes in grief.

"I want to send flowers," Leah said. "Would roses be stupid?"

"No, of course not, only you don't usually send flowers. It's
not a Jewish custom. You send a basket of fruit or something.
Or you take food. Or . . ."

"So we can't . . ."

"Actually, I don't know. Rose wasn't Jewish, but Jack is. I
know because one time Rose and I both took a handling seminar
sometime around Christmas, and Vera—that was her last poodle, before Caprice—had on one of those Christmas collars.
With lights? It's a regular collar, but it has little green and red
lights. They're powered by a little battery in the collar, and they
twinkle off and on."

"Isn't that dangerous?"

"No. It's only a nine-volt battery or something. Anyhow,
when Rose walked in, Vera had on this collar, which wasn't exactly like putting up a Christmas tree, but . . . Anyway, they
did both, Christmas and Hanukkah, or maybe he didn't do
Christmas, but she did both. Besides, her name was Rose
Marie."

"So?"

"So Marie is not a very common Jewish name."

"Maybe she was half Jewish."

"I don't think so, because his family wouldn't have minded so much then, or at least I don't think they would've, and they did. When he married Rose, his family sat shiva for him. You know what that means? For them, it was as if he'd died. Shiva is mourning. The family stays home for a week, to mourn. People bring food for them, and they visit, and, you know, pay their respects. It's instead of a wake or visiting hours or whatever."

"With the body right there? Yuck."

I shook my head. "For Orthodox Jews, the funeral has to be right away, within twenty-four hours. This is after."

"Is Jack doing that?"

"I don't know." I expected her to ask how we could avoid going, but she looked brighter-eyed than she had since I'd told her about Rose's death.

"If he is," she asked, "can we go?"

"Sure," I said. "I'm sure he'd appreciate it. And I'll ask around and make sure it's okay, but if you want to take roses, or send them, I don't think there's anything wrong with that. We can do the traditional thing, too. We'll take food."

"There's a slight problem with that, isn't there?" She managed a quirky little smile. "You know."

"I know what?"

"That you don't cook, exactly."

"Relax," I said. "I know not to show up with homemade dog biscuits." Actually, why not? In her own way, Caprice was presumably sitting shiva, too. "Anyway, it's not such a bad idea."

"No!"

"We can buy something."

"Don't you even have a cookbook?"

"As a matter of fact," I said smugly, "I do." I retrieved it from a kitchen drawer and handed it to her. It was one of those spiral-bound compilations of everybody's favorite recipes, the kind of cookbook that PTAs sell to raise money, but this one hadn't come from a PTA. It was folded open, and I handed it to Leah that way.

She read incredulously: " 'Preparation H works wonders on those little cuts and scrapes your horse is always getting.' "

"You're in the wrong section," I said. "It's from a humane society. There's stuff for people somewhere."

She flipped pages. "Chicken salad, maybe? Unless it's *for* chickens."

"It isn't," I said. "Make a list."

But the sadness hit us again, and that time, we both cried and hugged the dogs. Later, we shopped and cooked together, and for once, I didn't mind and wasn't bored because, Leah and I decided, we weren't just cooking, but performing a ritual, one of the traditional rites of women. I also spent some time on the phone calling a few people who might not have heard and taking calls from others who wanted to make sure I had.

The ritual distracted Leah, but didn't, of course, answer her original questions. When Steve showed up at six and I told him what had happened, the first thing she asked him was how much it had hurt.

Steve is always gentle. "People say that first, they feel nothing," he told her. "That's what this uncle of mine says. He was out on his tractor and got hit by lightning. First he didn't feel a thing, and then it was like he got hit with a giant hammer. Sometimes there's total amnesia."

"Is he all right?" Leah asked.

"Reborn. His breathing stopped, heart stopped. Lightning death, it's called. But one of the guys revived him, right away. What can happen is that the heart starts again, but respiration doesn't, and then there's brain damage. But some people just recover. Anyway, he decided since he'd died and come back to life, it was a sign. So he swore off alcohol and tobacco. You could say it basically improved his health."

"So why did Rose . . . ?"

"If it was a direct strike, maybe. Not a shock, but a direct strike. What tends to happen is that people are either killed outright or they're stunned, like my uncle, and they make a full recovery, maybe because what they got was a shock, not the full force."

"But," I interrupted, "if it was because she was touching the metal fence . . . ?"

"So how much did it hurt her?" Leah persisted.

"If she'd lived, she might not have remembered it," Steve said. "Chances are real good that everything just stopped. Her heart stopped beating. She stopped breathing. Just like tha

His eyes were green and serious and fixed hard on Leah. "She did not lie there in pain. She did not struggle."

Her eyes filled with tears, but the tension left her face, and when Jeff Cohen called to invite her to a party in Newton, I could tell that she'd had enough of adult grief and adult explanation.

"It doesn't seem very, um, respectful," she said.

"Leah, Rose would not have minded," I assured her. "She'd be glad to hear that you cried for her and that you'll miss her, but you don't need to stay home. Do you want the car?"

"Is that okay?"

"Fine." One of the reasons I'd agreed to have her stay in the first place was that she did drive and wouldn't have to depend on me to ferry her around. "But take Kimi with you. Not to the party. Just leave her in the car, with the windows open enough so she gets air but nobody can get a hand in to reach the locks. If you get a flat or something, and you have to walk somewhere, you won't be alone." (At night, with the windows open, fine, but never, ever on a hot day—dogs are horribly vulnerable to heatstroke.)

After Leah left, I told Steve some things I hadn't wanted her to hear. "I keep worrying that she was burned, that when she reached out to the gate and touched it, what happened was like a horrible burn. I kept trying to tell Leah that she didn't feel anything, but it keeps eating at me. And not only that it hurt, but that it hurt in some really intense, gruesome way, like those scenes in movies, electrocutions. It seems like the worst way to die. You downplayed it to her. I know you did."

"In animals, it can shatter bones," he said reluctantly. "Teeth. Most of the time, you don't see burns or marks, but you can. It can be like I told her. But how do we know? We hear what people say if they survive. We don't hear the others. It is fast. That's true. And there can be amnesia, but not always. The truth is I think it can be excruciating. I'm sorry."

Chapter 7

WITH the rigid formality of adolescence, Leah dressed herself in only one layer of nonathletic black and wound the indomitable radiance of her hair into a subdued knot for our visit to Jack Engleman. In lieu of attending the Sunday morning funeral (do I need to make excuses? I *could not* go), I'd had a fancy basket of fruit delivered to the house. It was a poor substitute, I know, but Jack wanted the funeral small and the burial private, Bess had told me, and she'd suggested that we visit sometime in the late afternoon.

"Are you nervous about it?" I asked Leah as she artfully mounded the chicken salad on a platter of lettuce.

"No. Why would I be nervous?"

"I don't know. I thought maybe you'd be afraid everybody would be crying. Or you wouldn't know what to expect."

"I don't exactly know what to expect, but it won't be anything I can't handle," said Leah, a human malamute, after all.

("Projection," my friend and tenant Rita commented later. "You project a lot onto that kid. Just who was anxious?" Obviously, Rita is a therapist, and not the physical kind.)

On my way out to the car, I saw Kevin Dennehy attacking the scrubby row of barberry between his mother's yard and mine with a pair of rusty hedge trimmers. I once tried to talk Kevin into replacing the ugly, prickly stuff with something classy like hemlock or juniper, and I even offered to split the cost. He rejected the proposal, and although he never said so outright, I had the impression that I'd made a serious gaffe, like offering to pay for half of a new Audi to avoid the humiliation of having his Chevy visible from my kitchen window.

When he saw us, he quit stabbing the barberry and lumbered

over, holding the pruners with one hand and wiping the sweat
off his face with the other.

He rumbled in my ear in what was, I think, supposed to be
a whisper: "Can I have a word with you?" When Kevin lowers
his voice, he adjusts the pitch, not the volume. When I sent Leah
back inside to put out extra water for the dogs and make sure
the answering machine was on, he said, "The wake?"

We'd seen him on our way back from shopping, and I'd told
him about Rose.

"Sort of. Visiting the house."

"Pacemaker," he said.

"What?"

"Gadget implanted in her chest."

"I know what a pacemaker is. Rose had one? So that's
why . . . What's this secrecy business? A pacemaker isn't a treat-
ment for VD or something."

"Eliot Park," he said.

"Yes."

"You still going to dog school there?"

"I know what you're worried about. The graffiti, right? You
think there's some sinister connection with dog training at the
park, between dog training and the graffiti and what happened
to Rose. Well, the only connection is that Rose lived near the
park and trained her dog there, so she's the one who arranged
to have the club use it. If we'd never been there, she'd have been
training in the tennis courts. The club had nothing to do with
anything. But obviously her death was less of a freak accident
than we thought. I mean, a pacemaker? With water and electricity?"

He shrugged.

"Hey, how did you know that Rose had a pacemaker?"

But Leah came down the back stairs, and Kevin wagged his
big head back and forth. He apparently didn't want to discuss
an autopsy in front of her. He managed to lower the volume
of his voice for the duration of two syllables: "Inquest."

The woman who opened Jack Engleman's front door had
coarse salt-and-pepper hair swept away from the thick, moist
skin of her face, and short, stubby fingers with blunt nails. She
introduced herself as Charlotte Zager, told us she was Jack's
sister, and then grabbed my hand and twisted it as ferociously

as if it were a decayed molar with stubborn roots that was resist-
ing extraction. I wasn't surprised to learn that she was a dentist.

The smallest of the three or four baskets of fruit on the tables
in the hallway may have been ours, or maybe some of the apples
and pears piled in a great silver bowl on the living room coffee
table had come from the one I'd sent. Protestant death smells
like gladioli, Jewish death like fruit. The oddest thing about all
of those pineapples, all of the dozens of bunches of grapes and
bananas, and the hundreds of pears, grapefruit, oranges, and apples was that no one seemed to be eating any fruit at all. In the
dining room, people were helping themselves to bagels, lox,
cream cheese, and tomatoes, and some of the people in the hall
and living room were eating brownies and pastry, but everyone
was treating the fruit as if it were made of wax.

Rose's death had dimmed the glow of Jack's skin, and when
you looked in his eyes, it was easy to tell that he wasn't there.
Even so, he welcomed us. Had anyone spoken to him the word
Kevin had whispered to me? I felt shy and took his hand, but
Leah threw her arms around him and held him, then sat with
him on the long flower-print couch opposite the empty fireplace.
It seemed to me that he was comforted by her youth and that
with no sense of age at all, she offered him a timeless, immediate
grace that I'd have been glad to give if I'd known where to find
it—if I had it in me at all.

Then Heather marched in holding Caprice in her arms and
said rather loudly, "Holly, what do you think of a trophy? Nonantum's trial's November nineteenth. There's lots of time. People'll give. Everyone knew Rose."

She stretched an arm to the silver bowl, plucked out a pol-
ished Granny Smith, and drove large, gleaming incisors through
it. The apple made a loud crunch.

"What I have in mind," she added, pointing to the silver
bowl, "is something like that."

Caprice's bright black eyes sighted down the line of her out-
stretched arm as she wondered which piece of fruit she was supposed to retrieve.

"Vera won that." Bess Stein had been sitting on a love seat
talking quietly with Jack's sister, but a lifetime of training dogs
had made her intolerant of gross misbehavior in any species.
It had also taught her to read the minds of hypercompetitive
handlers. To Bess and me, Heather's intentions were as clear

as if she'd been a hungry terrier eyeing a thick steak: She meant that memorial trophy for the highest-scoring poodle in Utility, and not just any highest-scoring poodle, either. Especially with Rose dead, the top poodle was apt to be her own.

"You know," Bess added, almost as if changing the subject, "Rose was the most graceful, unassuming winner."

"She was very tough and very gentle," said a dark-haired, lanky young man I didn't know. "I'm Jim O'Brian. I did my student teaching with Rose. In other words, I lucked out."

As the rest of us were introducing ourselves, Charlotte Zager ushered in a couple of women who also turned out to have been colleagues of Rose's and who joined Jim in eulogizing her.

"She had that wonderful, wonderful voice," one of them said.

"Musical," someone agreed.

"You wanted to keep hearing it," the first woman said. "When you first met her, you'd almost think she was kind of a pushover, she was so quiet, so unassuming. But people found out soon enough! I think she was the most patient, persistent person I've ever met. And such an optimist! So *positive*. But talk about determined!"

And murdered? Determined and murdered.

"You remember the time she filed that 51A?" the other woman said. "Jack, you remember that."

He nodded absently.

"While I was with her," Jim O'Brian said. "Four years ago. This boy's parents were, you know, above reproach. As a matter of fact, they were copresidents of the PTA."

One of the other teachers opened her eyes wide and glared at him.

"Forget that," he said. "Let's say they were Mr. and Mrs. Newton. Anyway, it was the old story, bad bruises and worse explanations. And Rose spoke to them, suggested counseling. But it kept going on, and she went and filed a 51A." He saw our blank faces. "Suspicion of abuse."

"They mustn't have been any too pleased about that," said Charlotte Zager.

"Rose was not afraid of anger," Jack told her.

If she had been, I suppose, she'd never have married Jack. Or maybe whatever his family felt wasn't anger, but something else, maybe something quite different.

"Especially not if it had to do with children," someone said. "Or dogs. That was Rose. Children and dogs."

Jack's eyes filled with tears, and he put an arm around Leah.

"I'm doing everything we planned," she told him softly. "Kimi's going to get her C.D. this summer, just the way Rose said." My mother always used that same tone of voice to predict the canine future, as if it were preordained. Rose had led Leah not merely to want that C.D. but to expect it.

"Is that that malamute?" Heather asked. She laughed. No one else did.

"Yes," I said with an edge in my voice.

"Well, good luck. You'll need it." *Dog's Life* is always publishing articles about the importance of breeding for temperament. Heather's parents evidently hadn't subscribed.

After that, people talked in twosomes. Jim O'Brian wanted to hear about my malamutes and said he'd always wanted one. When I said I might be able to find him a nice rescue dog, he looked interested. We eventually said our good-byes. As I stood up, Charlotte Zager, who'd been showing people in and out as if it were her house, thanked me for the chicken salad and started to accompany me to the door, where Jack joined us. Charlotte stayed at the door, though, while he walked us to the car, which I'd parked on the street in front of the house next door. The louts we'd encountered last time were nowhere in sight. Leah was a few steps ahead of us when Charlotte called out: "Watch for the cab, Jack."

"My father's coming," he explained. "From Florida. He's eighty-five. He has never entered my house before." He paused. "Someone would've picked him up at the airport, but he insisted on the cab. God forbid that he should show a sign of weakness. First he takes a ride from us, then Charlotte decides he's helpless, next thing he ends up in a nursing home." Jack shrugged. "If he takes a cab, he's not helpless."

"He doesn't sound very helpless." I had to speak up because in the louts' yard a German shepherd—the older, darker one, the poor guy we'd seen slapped around—was growling and barking protectively at the end of a long rope. Want a dog with a really rotten temperament? In between whacking him, leave him tied up. It works every time. Anyway, the louts' front door opened and the youngest brother, Willie, the trainer of the other shepherd, appeared and hollered, "Kaiser, shut up! Dale, come get your dog." Then, catching sight of Leah, he ran his fingers through the hair on top of his head and ambled to the Bronco. I could see him talking to Leah.

"After all these years," Jack said, nodding toward the neighboring house, a nondescript yellow ark. "And they haven't so much as said a word. And this one, Willie, a student of Rose's. Not a word."

"Maybe they will." I frowned and shook my head sympathetically, doubting it.

When we reached the car, though, Willie stepped forward, held his hand out to Jack, and muttered almost apologetically, "Mr. Engleman, I'm sorry about Mrs. Engleman. I'm real sorry."

Chapter 8

"SOME of those people *would,* you know. They really would. They'd do anything. They just don't care." The speaker was Tamara Ryan, who has West Highland white terriers—Westies to their friends. She was talking about top obedience people, the real competitors. "Some of them actually would kill to win. I wouldn't put it past them at all."

Although Tamara and I were stretched out on the grass of Eliot Park with our backs resting against a tree, the expansive suburban evening air felt and smelled like the polluted miasma of a hermetically sealed kitchen in which someone was running the self-clean cycle of a heavily soiled oven. Sprawled on his back in the hope that a nonexistent breeze might fan his belly, Rowdy maintained a sour, stolid expression. It was too hot for him to bother chasing the Westies and too hot for them to bother provoking him. Rowdy and I had already had our individual turn with Tony, and it was so hot, we'd skipped the jumps. My skin felt greasy, and sweat was dribbling down my neck.

"And," Tamara went on, "the Donovans swear up and down that lightning did not strike."

"The people with the English cocker?" I asked. "Davy, right?" I remembered because I'd noticed on the list Nonantum had mailed after last week's class that these people had given the dog their own last name. If I name a dog Holly's Fuzzy Wuzzy or Winter's Arctic Storm or whatever, fine. That's normal. But an English cocker named David Donovan? When it comes to dogs, some people get carried away.

She nodded.

"How do they know?"

"They live right over there," said Tamara, pointing toward
the park entrance. "The yellow Victorian with the coral trim.
And they were home, too. Ask her. There she is. Lisa?"

Lisa Donovan turned out to be a tan, athletic-looking young
woman in white shorts and a green Izod shirt. She had a round,
smiling face and straight blond Dutch-boy hair.

"I was just saying you were home Friday night," Tamara told
her, "and you didn't hear lightning strike, you or Bill."

Lisa's face turned serious. She sat cross-legged on the ground
next to Rowdy and ran a hand over his head. "Shedding," she
remarked.

"Just beginning," I said.

"Yeah, we were home. We had guests. And you know what's
odd? The house has lightning rods. If it'd hit near here, wouldn't
it've hit them? I asked the police, but they're a lot of help. When
we got broken into, they said they knew who did it, and did they
catch him? No. So I ask a simple question like, 'If we've got
lightning rods, isn't it going to strike us first?' and they clam
up."

"Maybe they didn't know, either," I said out of loyalty to
Kevin, who complains that people don't want to tell the police
anything and then expect them to know everything.

"Oh, they knew," she said suspiciously. "They just weren't
saying."

I tried to get her off the police and back to the lightning. "If
it hit here, wouldn't you hear it? Or notice *something*?"

"Naturally, we heard thunder. Who didn't?" She was
scratching Rowdy's flanks and gathering bits of his white undercoat into a little ball. "And before the rain started, we sat out
back, and there was a lot of that whatever you call it, sheet lightning? Heat lightning? That overall kind, where there's a big,
even flash. And, sure, we heard some crashing and cracking,
but not practically next door. And wouldn't we have felt it? I
call that very peculiar."

I was about to call it pretty peculiar myself when she switched
the subject. Holding up Rowdy's fur and rubbing it between her
fingers, she asked, "You save this?"

"No."

"One of my neighbors would love it, is why I asked. She's
a weaver. She's into natural fibers. You want me to ask her
about it?"

"I guess so." The prospect of wearing Rowdy or Kimi felt repulsive. Then I had another thought. "Actually, does she make things?"

"Sure."

"My father would love that. A scarf or something. Would you ask her about it?"

"Yeah. Or maybe you know her. She has a border collie."

"Is her name Cohen?"

But that would have been too much of a coincidence.

"Marcia Brawley. I'll ask her. I'll let you know."

Then Tony Doucette, dapper in spite of the heat in a 1930s pre-air-conditioning seersucker suit, summoned us for the group exercises. Instructors like Tony are practically as eager to see their students make it into the ribbons and put titles on their dogs as the students are themselves. They want you to show, and even when you don't do anything more than qualify, they congratulate you in front of everyone, and they keep goading you and everyone else to get out there.

"Any brags tonight?" he asked when we'd lined up and sat our dogs. "No one? Come on!"

"Guilford," called out Heather. "High in trial. One ninety-seven plus."

"What'd they give you?"

"Pewter tray." She sounded disappointed.

"Who was the judge?"

"Martori," she said.

Samuel Martori, I would like to comment, once gave Vinnie, the best obedience dog I'll ever own, a humiliating 187 for a spectacular performance in Open for which she deserved a minimum of 199 plus. I had not shown under the bastard since.

Tamara and one of the Westies were next to us. "I will not show under him," she said quietly. "I was so glad to see him get that reprimand."

"So was I," I agreed.

In case you didn't know, the Secretary's Pages of *Pure-Bred Dogs/The American Kennel Gazette* make the most gossipy reading in dogdom, because that's where the AKC publishes notices of suspensions, reprimands, registration cancellations, and fines. Some of the notices are about boring, trivial stuff like clubs that were late sending in reports, but others are about unspecified—but obviously underhanded—"conduct in connection with" shows and trials. Every once in a while, there's a juicy line or two about what the culprit did. The notice about Martori stated that he'd accepted hospitality from an exhibitor before and after a trial he'd judged. What the *Gazette* didn't say, but what I'd heard from about a dozen people, was that he'd given the exhibitor a score in the 190s even though the dog ticked the high jump and didn't look as if it even had any idea how to sit straight. A history of ethical violations won't necessarily stop people from showing under a judge, though. What stopped other people from showing under Martori was the same thing that stopped me: unfair scoring, and not unfairly high, either.

Tamara leaned toward me and said, "You know, Rose was the one who turned him in."

"No!" I said.

I almost missed Tony's commands to sit and leave the dogs. In Open, the handlers have to go out of sight of the dogs for the sits and downs, and while we waited on the sidewalk just outside the park wall for Tony to call us back—or for someone to come and tell us that our dogs were up—Tamara and some other people kept insisting that Rose had been the person principally responsible for the reprimand.

"What did Rose do?" I asked.

"Complained in writing," Lisa said. "Her dog had a limp, so she wasn't competing, but she was there, and she saw how the dog did. And then she heard what the score was, and she ran into him while he was leaving with these people, and she hit the roof and complained in writing."

"Everyone at Nonantum knew about it," Tamara told me. "You just didn't know because you weren't training here."

"I knew about the reprimand," I said. "I just didn't know about Rose. If I had, I would've thanked her." I was about to ask Heather why she showed under Martori, but someone appeared and told me that Rowdy was shifting around and said Tony wanted to know if I wanted to do anything about it. I did.

To make sure that Rowdy didn't pull the same trick or a worse one on the long down, I walked away with the other handlers, but instead of following them out of the park, I stepped behind a tree where I could keep an eye on him. He rested his head morosely on his paws and didn't budge. He knew where I was.

Heather's daughter, Abbey, was sitting in a folding chair near the tree. She'd been observing the entire thing.

"There's a quick cure for that," she said.

I looked interested. Rowdy was restless because he was hot and wanted to go home, but if Abbey knew a trick, I wanted to hear what it was. One thing dog training teaches you is that you never know it all.

"Electronics," she said. "Give him a good zap, and that's one problem you won't have anymore."

"Yeah, I've heard." I tried to sound neutral. How other people train their dogs is none of my business, and there's nothing I can do about it, anyway.

On the way home, though, I lost it, and Leah got the full diatribe.

"You mean they give electric shocks to their dogs?" Leah was properly horrified. "Isn't that illegal or anything?"

"No, but it ought to be," I said. "That's what I think."

Okay, so once in a while, there's some desperate problem, and nothing else works. Suppose you've got a lot of dogs, and one of them keeps attacking one of the others, and you've tried everything else. You do obedience with both of the dogs. You keep them separate. You do everything right. And it happens again. And you *know,* you just *know,* that what's coming next is that the dog that's getting attacked is going to get torn up or killed one of these days, and probably you've already been bitten separating them because you didn't want to see the victim get hurt again. Okay, maybe then. *Maybe.* But for another couple of points in the ring? Come on.

"And," I went on, "the companies that sell these things are big business. You should see the brochures. I've got some at home. I'll show you one I really hate. It makes me so furious: There's a malamute on the cover. A malamute!"

"God!" Leah said.

Demi, at the very least. She was learning fast.

"You won't believe the ads and the brochures! I mean, they're totally professional, obviously done by some Madison Avenue outfit. I just hate them."

They never, ever use the words *electric* or *shock.* They sell "remote trainers," not shock collars. They really are remote. Some of the expensive new ones have a range of up to a mile. You can be a mile away from the dog, and when you press that button on the transmitter, he still gets a shock, and it can last for ten seconds, which is a long time for pain. That's another word they don't use. And when you up the voltage, you're "changing the level of stimulation." I'd like to stimulate whoever invented those damned things.

Chapter 9

LEAH was sitting opposite me at the kitchen table in the chair that's supposed to be empty when I'm working. She looked up from *Sense and Sensibility.* "What are you writing about?"

"Tail spraining." Wanna make something of it, kid?

She blinked.

"I know it wasn't a favorite subject of Jane Austen's," I said, "but she probably didn't have a mortgage and two dogs."

"She probably just didn't know about it," Leah said politely. "What do you have against Jane Austen?"

"Nothing. I like her." Of course, she wasn't Jack London, but not everyone hears the call of the wild.

It was Wednesday morning, and although the column wasn't due for a week, I was behind on my self-imposed beat-the-deadline schedule. Since Leah's arrival, I hadn't touched any of the articles I was working on, either, including a promising one about a computerized dating service for single dog-owners and an evaluation I'd promised to do of an apartment dwellers' device called the Doodoo Voodoo Box. Part of the problem was that Rita, my friend and tenant, had refused to fill out the dating service questionnaire, and Groucho, her dachshund, had started digging in the box instead of fouling it. Leah was another part of the problem.

"Not to mention your own part," Rita said later. I have told you that she's a psychologist, haven't I? "Consisting," she went on, "of your favorite transference relationship, namely, a tendency to shape your experiential reality in your mother's image, compounded in this instance by acute, self-generated sibling rivalry. In other words, you convinced yourself that Leah was more your own mother's daughter than you are and, further-

more, that your dogs knew it. For example, consider your per-
ception of her supposedly special relationship with Jack
Engleman, who, not incidentally, had just become a widower—
in other words, more and more like your father—plus, of course,
your readiness to blame her for interrupting your intimate relationship with Steve. The less transferential option open to you
was to go to her and say, 'Look, Leah, I can't write when you're
around, so go take a walk. And when you get back, Steve'll be
here, and he'll be staying all night.' "

My own interpretation differed slightly from Rita's. In wolf
packs, it seemed to me, juveniles were too busy chasing and
pouncing on each other to pester the adults, who were thus free
to stalk musk-oxen, win each other's favors, and otherwise do
their canine equivalents of writing their articles and sleeping
with their vets. I'd made what Rita would call my intervention
on Monday morning. "Maybe you'd like to have some people
over," I'd said. "Jeff? And anybody you met at that party." As
Rita pointed out, then, it was my own soft howl that first incited
the pups to gather. On Monday night, when I returned from
interviewing a guy in Arlington about the dating service, the
juvenile pack had established itself in my living room in front
of Rita's VCR, borrowed for the evening. On Tuesday, Leah
had called all of her new packmates, each of whom had called
her at least once. When we got back from dog training on Tuesday night, my answering machine had messages for Leah from
Ian, Seth, Miriam, Noah, Monica, and Emma, and didn't have
one from Jeff only because he'd been at dog training with us.
I quit answering the phone. Not one of the calls was for me.

Shortly after I explained what tail spraining was, the bell
rang. When I opened the front door, a happy-looking kid holding a big glass vase of long-stemmed red roses asked, "Winter?"

Nobody sends me flowers.

"Yes," I said, "but, uh, there's a mistake here. We *sent* roses.
They were supposed to go to someone else." In fact, I'd had
them sent to the funeral home on Saturday and had assumed
that Jack had thanked Leah during their tête-à-tête. "The names
must've got mixed up. Damn, that means they never . . ."

The kid read from a slip: "Leah Whitcomb, care of Winter,
two fifty-six Concord."

Her parents? Maybe normal parents do things like that. It's
always hard for me to guess. Not that Marissa was stingy, or

that Buck is, either, but, for one thing, Marissa loved flowers and hated to see them cut, and Buck never gives anyone anything except guns, dogs, fishing rods, and relevant accessories, none of which can be sent FTD.

But the roses weren't a mistake and weren't from her parents. They were from Willie Johnson, the youngest lout.

"What is this white stuff they're in? It looks like ice." Awe filled Leah's voice. She was delighted.

"Plastic, probably. Some kind of mush that retains moisture."

"Aren't they wonderful?"

"They're very romantic," I said. "I didn't know . . ."

"He's called a couple of times."

"But how did he know . . . ?"

"From the list," she said. The list of people in dog training, of course. "Remember?"

I counted the roses. There were a dozen. I wanted to ask Leah whether she knew how much a dozen long-stemmed roses cost, but I didn't.

"I guess I should call and say thank you."

"I guess you should," I said. Marissa always drilled me on the fine points of show ring and social etiquette. "Or you could write a note, I guess. Isn't that what Jane Austen would've done?"

Leah grinned. "I think I'll call."

When she finally got off the phone, she took Kimi outside to train her, and I called Steve, who was a little irked.

"Just leave her and come over," he said. "What's going to happen?"

"She's only sixteen," I said, "and I don't know these kids, except Jeff, and what if this one shows up? I don't want her alone with him. He must be at least two or three years older than she is, and you should see the way he leers at her. Maybe he's a perfectly nice kid, but she looks older than she is, and I don't know him, and I'm not all that crazy about what I've seen. And, look. Weird stuff is happening. I need to talk to you. Anyway, I need to be here."

"And if he asks her out?" Steve said. "You intend to tell her no?"

"I don't know. I should've got this straight to begin with. When Jeff appeared, I thought I wasn't going to have to worry

about limits like that. Anyway, I don't know what she's doing
tonight. Maybe Jeff will call, but I don't want all the rest of them
here when I'm not home. Half an hour or something, okay, but
not the whole evening. And I don't want her here alone. Look,
these roses are sort of out of line. I mean, he's seen her maybe
four times. At two classes, at the match the other night, and
then on Sunday, at Jack Engleman's. And apparently he's called
her, but that's it. And now he sends these incredibly expensive
flowers. I don't like it. It feels off."

"So what does she think?"

"Oh, she's thrilled. Anyway, come over. Maybe she'll go out,
or maybe she'll stay in her room and read Jane Austen."

"And we'll stay in yours, and I'll read you anything you
want."

"Look, Steve, I'm serious. I need to talk. It's about Rose Engleman. People are saying things, and Kevin told me there's an
inquest. He let it drop, and then when I asked him about it yes-
terday, he said he didn't know any more about it. And that's
probably true, because he's Cambridge, and that's Newton.
Anyway, we need to talk, and not on the phone."

"It's because I didn't send roses, isn't it?" he said. "If I bring
them with me, will you get rid of her?"

"Please! And if you want to bring something, stop at McDonald's and get me a fish sandwich, a chocolate shake, garden salad
with Ranch. And some fries. And get a Quarter Pounder with
cheese, and a salad, and diet something for Leah, and whatever
you want."

But he showed up with human Eukanuba, premium-quality
chow, which is to say, frozen gourmet take-out stuffed sole in
aluminum trays, mussel and shell salad, three-dollar-a-loaf
French bread, one of those dark-chocolate cakes made with
heavy cream and no flour, and a bottle of white Burgundy. Jeff
called to see if Leah wanted to go to the Square—she did—and
just as she finished eating a two-thousand-calorie wedge of cake
with a glass of diet iced tea, I heard him at the back door. When
I pulled it open, he was smirking. His hands were behind his
back. He followed me into the kitchen, nodded to Steve, and
gave a half-shy but elaborately sweet imitation of a magician
as he presented Leah with a bunch of daisies and mums that
probably came from a supermarket, but were pretty, anyway,

and would undoubtedly last a lot longer than the roses, which were, fortunately, in her room.

"Nice kid," Steve said when they left.

"Very," I agreed. "You know, when he calls, he actually talks to me? And not in that sort of stiff, pseudo-adult way you get when kids suddenly turn on the manners, either. I can't believe that with him around, she'd really be interested in the other one, roses or no roses. He's . . . I don't know. What can I say? You take one look at him, and you don't want your sixteen-year-old cousin going out with him. He's probably all right, but you just don't."

"You want some advice?"

"Sure."

"Don't say that to her."

"I know better than that," I said. "I should probably tell her that you and I are both crazy about Willie and don't trust Jeff, right?"

"Do we?" He reached over and cupped my chin in his hand. "Come on."

"You come on," he said gently. "Or did someone else send you roses?"

A while later, when we were back in the kitchen finishing the cake and the Burgundy, I said, "Can we talk now?"

"Sure," he said.

"Actually, first, I want to talk, and I want you to listen, okay? Because between Leah, and not getting any work done, and the heat and everything, I'm not thinking too clearly. Okay? And then I want you to tell me everything you know about pacemakers."

"Not a lot."

"Fine," I said. "Then just listen. First of all, it's obvious that the autopsy showed something, or maybe it failed to show something. For instance, maybe it showed that lightning didn't hit her. I don't know. Autopsy results aren't public."

"Her husband will know."

"Why?"

"Because they'll have told him. In a case like that, the family's informed."

"Are you sure?"

"Pretty sure. You could ask him."

"How?" I said. "What am I going to say? 'Gee, Jack, people

are saying that Rose was murdered, and I wondered if I could see your copy of the autopsy report because I'm low on bedtime reading and . . .'?"

"Are people saying that?"

"In a way. Some of what I heard was just kind of frivolous. You know how people talk about the top handlers. First of all, everybody resents them, mostly just because they win, but also because some of them have a bad attitude. They're arrogant. And some judges *do* let them bend the rules. Mostly, though, people who basically want to have fun resent it when the whole thing gets turned into a high-pressure contest."

Steve has a shepherd bitch who has her C.D.X.—Companion Dog Excellent—and with good scores, too. He knew what I meant. "It's real boring when that happens."

"So you know how people say that some of those people really would do *anything*? I've said it myself. So people are saying that, and maybe this time, it isn't just . . . It's possible that this time, someone did. Nobody who doesn't show dogs would believe that anyone would do something like that, but if you do, then you know, honest to God, it is possible."

"There've been a couple of cases where dogs were poisoned at shows."

"But those were all in breed, weren't they? Because in breed, if you killed the handler, the owner would just hire someone else. Or if you killed the owner, someone else would go on showing the dog. It wouldn't do you any good to kill a person. But in obedience, your real competition isn't the person or the dog. It's the team. But I just can't see obedience people doing it. In breed, the dogs are more like objects—but obedience? So maybe a rare person, a really competitive handler, will do something awful, like step on your dog's toes."

"Jesus!"

"But I really think that most obedience people would rather kill a person than a dog. And besides, it isn't the dogs anyone resents. It's the handlers."

"Is there some particular handler you have in mind?"

"Yes," I said. "Heather Ross. You know who she is."

"Silver hair? With the silver standard poodle."

"Yeah."

"Rose Engleman was that much of a threat to her?"

"Well, probably from her point of view. For one thing, Rose

also had poodles, and they'd been sort of archrivals for years. Poodle people are always so competitive. They have such high standards, because poodles can be such incredible obedience dogs. Malamute people aren't like that, not in obedience."

He laughed.

"Well, okay. In obedience, we practically never even see each other, especially around here. The only malamutes you ever see in obedience around here are mine, but the point is, I wouldn't, and other malamute people wouldn't, either, because they obviously aren't the world's greatest obedience dogs."

"Misery loves company," he said.

"It's sort of true. When I see that someone's put a U.D. on a mal—yes, it actually has been done—I feel grateful that somebody proved it's possible, and I know how much agony went into it. But there are millions of poodles in obedience, and they aren't as easy to train as people say. You have to work hard, and then even when your dog is really good, you've got lots of competition. With a poodle, anything below one ninety or one ninety-five is a disgrace, or that's what they think, which is why they're the people you see painting the backs of their shoes to match the dog."

"What?"

"It's an old trick. If you think the dog's going to sit a little crooked, and you've got a black dog, you make sure the backs of your shoes are black, so the judge won't notice if the sit's a little off. I don't do that, but with Rowdy, I always wear a dark skirt, and I never wear anything with a line down the front, a row of buttons or anything the judge could use to line up on and see if he sits just slightly crooked. That's fair enough. It's not like taping a hunk of raw liver to your left thigh."

"Jesus!"

"You laugh! People do it. Anyway, how did we end up talking about dogs? Here's what I know about Heather. First of all, since she'd known Rose for years, she probably knew she had a pacemaker. I didn't see Rose all that often, but Heather did, since they both belong to Nonantum. Rose was showing the signs of some kind of heart trouble and then was in the hospital and then got better, so Heather must've known. Second, obviously, she benefits. She's already started planning a memorial trophy that she can win. It's disgusting. And the other thing is that according to the people who live across the street from the park, lightning didn't strike there. They were home. And they say it didn't hit. So what did? It's raining. Rose is probably standing in a puddle of water. She has a pacemaker. She reaches out and touches the gate, and it's metal. And something happens."

"And? You don't sound like you're done."

"And, look. Heather isn't the only one who gained, and with the pacemaker, Rose was vulnerable, more vulnerable than most people. That's what's bothering me most, I think. A lot of things can screw up a pacemaker, and a lot of people had something against her. Like Jack's family. She wasn't Jewish, and when he married her, they sat shiva. And then at the house, his sister was there, and his father was arriving, and it felt like a sort of family reunion. And there are other people, people who had some kind of case against her. One is that son of a bitch Martori, the judge. You know who he is? She got him reprimanded. And there were these other people she accused of child abuse. Anyhow, the fact is, there were a lot of people who weren't happy to have her alive."

Chapter 10

I woke up the next morning with Heather, Abbey, and double handling on my mind. Obedience competition, it seemed to me, is a game that combines a giant version of bridge with an elaborate form of solitaire. You have a partner, so do lots of other players, and one of your aims is to do better than they do, but your main contest is the one you play with yourself. Double handling is as dirty as cheating at cards and as pointless as cheating at solitaire, which is not to say that it's easy, especially if it's as smooth as Heather and Abbey's.

Rowdy was sleeping on the floor under the rattly old Hotpoint portable air conditioner, but before I opened my eyes, I heard him stir, and a couple of seconds later, I could feel him staring at me. You may be able to convince your spouse, your lover, or even your children that you're still asleep when you're not, but you can't fool a dog.

"Good morning, buddy," I said.

He wagged his entire rear end and made that funny face malamutes put on when they'd like to bark like normal dogs, but don't remember how. Then he woo-wooed at me, and I gave up and got up. When I'd let him out and in, measured out exactly one cupful of ANF30, put it in his bowl, and watched him devour half of it before the bowl hit the floor, I stood there in the kitchen and thought about malamutes and Jews, about my own family and Leah's, and about Jack Engleman's—in other words, about insiders and outsiders. Before that odd early morning moment, I'd assumed that no one with four WASP grandparents could grasp Jack's family's response to Rose and their marriage, but it came to me that the relationship between Leah's parents and my own was in some ways as if they had sat shiva for each other. From my parents' viewpoint, the problem with Arthur—and Cassie, ever since she married him—wasn't anything he'd done, anything personal. The real issue was that we were dog people, but Arthur belonged to another clan. All of the personal gripes stemmed from that radical objection: He wasn't one of us. Well, so what?

This is where malamutes and Jews come in, and don't be offended. I'm serious. To my way of thinking, you see, the Alaskan malamute is, honest to God, God's chosen dog, and no matter how much I love and admire dogs of any and all other breeds, I don't want my malamutes jeopardizing the identity of their clan, because if enough of them do, there won't be any clan anymore. How come? Because malamutes are so much better than other dogs? As bird dogs, guard dogs, or lapdogs, they're useless, and if you try to get a mal to herd sheep, he'll herd them directly into his stomach. A golden retriever, sheltie, German shepherd, poodle, border collie, or the average specimen of fifty or sixty other breeds, not to mention the average all-American mixed breed dog, is a better obedience prospect than the average malamute. Siberian huskies are faster racing dogs, bloodhounds track better than malamutes do, and if I ever lost my sight, even I wouldn't trust a mal as a guide dog. Superior? No. Just different. Wonderful. Special. Chosen. And don't think I'm confusing dogs with people, either. I don't know whether Jews are different from other people, but that's not the point. What I understood was the feeling people have about belonging to a clan and the importance people can attach to preserving it. I wouldn't have bred Rowdy to Vinnie, my best golden ever, and there wouldn't have been anything personal about it. Is it fair to have the same attitude toward people? I didn't know, but I was beginning to understand the feeling.

"So," I said to Rowdy, "the hypothetical situation is this: You get loose and fall hopelessly in love with a golden retriever. You won't look at another mal, refuse to come home, and you father a litter of mixed breed pups. How do I feel? Okay, angry. It may be silly, but I can't help it. And since we're talking about people, let's magnify it a lot, because the fact is, I could always get some more dogs, but children are hard to replace. And do I want your mate dead? Am I angry enough to kill her? If it's the only way I get you back? Of course not. I don't want anything enough to kill a dog." But not everyone feels that way about dogs. Or about other people.

Half an hour later, when Rita stopped in for coffee, I told her what I'd been thinking about, and she told me not to do what I've just done, namely, tell anyone.

"Holly, look," she said emphatically. "I never give advice. Hardly ever. But I'm telling you, don't say any of this to anyone else, okay? I know you, and I understand that you're not kidding. Dogs are how you understand Arabs, the Mideast situation, feminism, the Holy Trinity, psychotherapy, higher education, and everyone and everything else, but I'm telling you, you need to be aware that most people are going to find this frivolous and offensive, and you need to keep it to yourself. If it ever comes up, just say that you think you can empathize a little, or whatever. Don't mention dogs."

"Well, I won't mention them to Charlotte Zager," I promised.

"Who?"

"Jack Engleman's sister. Charlotte Zager. She's cleaning my teeth this afternoon."

"What?"

"Well, she *is* a dentist," I said.

In the midafternoon, I was sitting in a blue plastic stackable chair in a yellow plastic office in Newton Centre. I was trying to fill out the patient information form handed me on a clipboard by the receptionist. The form asked how I was referred to Dr. Zager, and it seemed inappropriate to write that I'd met her while visiting her brother when his gentile wife had just died under suspicious circumstances, that it was the first time Dr. Zager had been in the house, because the family sat shiva for Jack when he married Rose, that Dr. Zager seemed to me to be making herself all too at home there all of a sudden, and that I wondered what kind of person she was and couldn't think of any easier way to pursue an acquaintance with a dentist than to get my teeth cleaned. Besides, there wasn't room on the form.

The memory of Charlotte Zager's molar-wrenching handshake made me a little nervous, but after an assistant showed me into an examining room, put a bib around my neck, and cranked me up in a reclining dental chair, Dr. Zager came in, remembered me, didn't ask any weird questions about how I happened to be there, and said she'd check my teeth when the hygienist finished cleaning them. Although I'd seen my own hygienist only a month earlier, this one, a pickle-mouthed blonde who delivered a moralistic scolding about regular flossing, spent half an hour lacerating my gums. When she finally tore her gloves off, Charlotte Zager came back and took a remarkably gentle look.

"Holly," she pronounced, "I think your teeth can be saved."

In case you think she was kidding, you should know that my father considers fluoride to be one of the principal instruments of the communist conspiracy. My teeth are a cold-war battlefield. Charlotte Zager was the Gorbachev of dentistry. She made me chomp into a mass of nauseating wax and told me I'd get a call when my fluoride trays came back from the lab and that when they did, the hygienist would show me how to use them. Then she asked whether I had a dog.

"Two," I said.

"You do know about caring for their teeth?" she said. "They have teeth, too, you know."

The most recent proof I bore of the truth of her claim was a scar left by Kimi, but I didn't hold up my hand and point to it. It was mostly my own fault, and people don't always understand that Kimi didn't mean it. (I never tell people that if she'd been serious, I wouldn't have the hand at all.)

"I do try to brush their teeth," I said.

If this sounds bizarre, you're behind the canine times. These days, the well-groomed Rover has his own toothbrush and special toothpaste that's safe to swallow. If he suffers from halitosis, he also gets his gums squirted with mouthwash glop, and if he's lucky, he gnaws on a bone-shaped hunk of dental floss.

"And regular professional cleaning?" she asked.

"No," I said. "They're both fairly young, and their teeth are good, and I don't think it's worth the risk of the general anesthetic." Ready for a historic first? I swear, it was the first time I'd even considered this question, never mind actually uttered it, and the words felt stranger in my mouth than the lingering taste of wax: "Um, why are we talking about dogs?"

It might have been a first for me, but not for her. "My son is a veterinarian."

And does he always ask his patients about their owners'

teeth? But I didn't say it. "Oh, what's his name? I have a good friend who's a vet."

"Don," she said.

"Zager?"

She nodded.

"Is he around here?"

"Newtonville," she said. "On Washington Street."

On my way home, I took a slight detour to satisfy my curiosity. Not far from the corner of Walnut Street was a shabby two-story house with a curtained storefront and a fresh white shingle that showed a stylized outline of a Scottie and the name Donald M. Zager, D.V.M. The dumpy faded building had a view of the section of the Mass. Pike that has a Star Market built over it. It reminded me of something Rose Engleman had said, that Newton isn't the way people think it is. As I know from Steve, who hates the business part of being a vet, even someone with great credentials and an endearing whelping-box manner has to remember that owners care about appearances even if the patients don't. Donald Zager's clinic looked like a place you'd go to have your palm read or your cards done, not somewhere you'd want your dog neutered or your cat defleaed.

Chapter 11

"Just give it back," Jeff was telling Leah when I walked in. His tone was reasonable, but his expression was hurt and sullen. The humidity had made deep-golden ringlets of his hair. He looked like a gawky, pissed-off Renaissance angel.

Leah's hair was meticulously French-braided in cornrows and plaits, but an aura of tendrils had escaped. Her eyes were pleased, her mouth stubborn.

"No," she said forcefully. "Why should I?"

One of them might at least have said hello to me. I flashed them a post dental-hygienic smile, anyway.

Jeff nodded to me and mumbled. He looked abashed. "I've got to go," he said. "See ya."

"So what's this about?" I asked Leah when the door closed behind him. She was standing mule-like in the middle of the kitchen. "Or maybe it's none of my business."

"Nothing," she said. He's just making . . . Forget it."

"Oh, damn. He noticed the roses."

"Not exactly."

"What does that mean?"

"Not the roses. It was something else."

"Willie, uh, sent something else?"

"Brought it."

I looked around the kitchen, but there weren't any flowers. "Well, what was it? And what is he giving you stuff for? He practically doesn't even know you."

"So?"

"So what is it?"

She produced what used to be called a boom box—I'm not sure what the right word is now—a supersize combination

69

radio, tape, and CD player with a few dozen dials and lights and big detachable speakers, the kind of contraption that runs through ten D batteries every few hours. It was even bigger than the one she had and much flashier.

"It looks like the one in that Spike Lee movie," I said. "You know, the one that kid carries around. And then it gets kicked in."

"Wait'll you hear it!"

"When I walked in, Jeff was telling you to give it back."

She smiled and made a face.

"I hate to tell you," I said, "but the fact is, you do have to give it back. Tough, but there you have it."

When malamutes decide they don't want to do something, they plant their feet, brace their legs, and imitate the Central Park statue of Balto, the canine hero of the 1925 Great Serum Run that saved Nome from diphtheria. I wasn't sure whether Leah was imitating the statue of Balto or imitating Kimi and Rowdy's imitation, but she locked her knees and elbows, clenched her jaw, and froze that way.

"The best thing would be," I went on, "if you call him and explain. You don't have to be rude or anything. All you do is say you can't take such a big present. I know you think it's wonderful and you want to keep it. But you can't."

"That is not fair! And what's he supposed to . . . ?"

"Leah, he didn't know any better, that's all. Among other things, it's no favor to him to let him think this is just sort of the way it's done, because it isn't. You can ask Rita if you want. Or we can try to call your parents. Or look it up in Miss Manners."

"I think you're being a snob," she said, but at least she said something.

"You know Kevin Dennehy, right? Is he a snob?"

She shook her head.

"Well, if we need an arbiter, or you'd feel better if we got a sort of second opinion, we can tell Kevin about it, but I'm warning you, he'd probably ram it down the kid's throat or bash him over the head with it. And he won't demand to know the gentleman's intentions, either. He'll assume he knows what they are."

She looked stunned. "That is the stupidest . . . Nobody would . . ."

"Kevin would," I said. "And I agree tha[t]
chaic. Look, Leah, it'd be just as out of li[ne]
something like this. Can you imagine do[ing]
people are easier than dogs. Try getting a n[ew]
roles and see the other dog's point of view. "Ke[vin]
going out and spending hundreds and hundreds on so[mething]
like this and giving it to somebody you've met a couple of tim[es]
You just wouldn't do it, right? No matter how much you
wanted the person to like you, you'd know that that wasn't the
way to do it. It wouldn't even occur to you, but if it did, it would
feel strange, and you'd find some other way to meet whoever
it was."

She burst into tears. "What am I supposed to do? Write him
a letter and say, 'Sir, ladies do not accept blah blah blah, and
my aunt doubts the purity of your . . .'?"

"Do you want *me* to take it back?"

Her look was relieved and suspicious.

"I'll be nice about it," I promised. "I'll say how generous it
was, which it was. I know it would be hard for you, and it's
no big thing for me. You want me to?"

She nodded. "Would you?"

I returned the nod. "Look, did you remember to take the dogs
out? And run a brush through them, would you? And when you
do, put the fur in a plastic bag. I'm going to . . . Never mind.
I'll tell you about it later. And then vacuum in here, or there'll
be fur in everything we eat. I'll be back soon."

The Bronco made it back over the great suburban divide and
to the Johnsons' house in only twenty minutes. If I had three
muscular kids and a big house in Newton, or even if I just had
the house, I wouldn't hire a lawn service, but the grass would
be cut the way the Johnsons' wasn't, and someone would dig
out the dandelions the way no one had uprooted theirs.

At first I thought no one was home. Old-fashioned non-mini,
wide-slatted aquamarine venetian blinds were lowered on all the
windows. The front door had a peephole, and mounted to the
right of the door, next to a lump of crisscrossed silver duct ta[pe]
that probably covered a doorbell, was a shabby intercom [with]
a collection of unlabeled buttons and switches. Above [it,]
cased in a plastic food-storage bag, hung a piece of ragge[d]
board on which someone had printed in black bloc[k]
"Beware of the dog." I rested the oversize brown sh[

ning the boom box on a dirty sisal mat that read: "Wel-
."

pushed some buttons on the intercom and, after a minute
two, rapped my knuckles on the door. Then I kept pressing
what I thought was the most likely button and spoke into the
little box: "Hello? Anyone home?"

One slat on the window to my right rose an inch or two and
then sank. I rapped on the door and tried to sound as if the sisal
mat meant what it said: "Hello? Anyone home?"

When I'm in the middle of writing something, I sometimes
just let my doorbell ring, too, because often enough, the stranger
standing there turns out to be a solicitor for Greenpeace or a
Jehovah's Witness. I knocked hard and called out, "Hello? Is
Willie there? My name is Holly Winter." Just in case the neighborhood was as heavily canvassed as mine, I yelled that I wasn't
collecting for anything. When the front door suddenly opened
inward, I found myself looking into the face of Willie's brother,
the one from the fun match, and hollering: "And I'm not a Jehovah's Witness!"

I felt like a jerk.

He must have caught only the last two words. "Mom isn't
interested," he said. "She's Presbyterian."

I hadn't seen the brother up close before. Like Willie, he had
white-blond hair, but the sides of Willie's head were shaved
bald. His brother's hair stood luxuriantly and stiffly on end all
over his head. His features were chunkier than Willie's, and his
expression was stupefied but vaguely bellicose.

"Um, I was saying I'm not," I told him. "I thought maybe . . .
Never mind. Could we start over? My name is Holly Winter.
Willie and I train dogs together. I need to see him. Is he here?"

He shook his head. Willie's brother didn't have shoulders like
Kevin Dennehy's, but he was working on them, and he was
taller and beefier than Willie, who was squat and stocky. In fact,
the brother had probably been building his lats or traps when
rang the bell: His white T-shirt and yellow shorts were soaked,
face flushed.

small gray-haired woman with the expression of a fright-
quirrel stood behind him and peered at me.

Johnson?" I said.

s opened in alarm, as if I were trying to scare her off
r.

"Mrs. John[...]
our dogs together[...]

She tilted her head[...]
"You want me let her [...] in?"

She jerked her bony little chin at [...]
and I carried the heavy bag in. Ev[...]
front entrance hall, the dining room[...]down, he [...]
room on the left, and the wide flight of st[...] I could see—[...]
was papered, painted, carpeted, or upholstered[...] right, the living
marine. The lowered blinds let in murky light. I f[...]ctly ahead—
just stepped into a giant aquarium.[...]ddy aqua-
[...] if I had

Dale abruptly lumbered off through the dining room, and I
heard the swish of a swinging door. Mrs. Johnson stood bewildered, wrapping the fingers of her left hand around the first finger of the right and squeezing hard. I had the sense that she'd
once known what to do next—invite me to sit down, ask me
what I wanted—and was hoping that, somehow, if she wrung
that finger painfully enough, the memory would squirt out.

"Willie's gone to Star Market for me," she said with some
alarm.

"Do you expect him back soon?"

Her mindless eyes opened into frightened circles.

I tried to sound matter-of-fact. "I just need to see him for
a second. Do you expect him back soon?"

She shrugged her shoulders as if I'd asked her the meaning
of life.

"How long ago did he leave?" I asked.

"An hour? An hour ago?"

Why ask me?

"Then he'll probably be back soon," I said. "Do you think
I could wait for him?"

She nodded and finally moved toward the living room. I followed her. She perched on the edge of a wing-back chair, and
I sat on the couch. I wasn't looking forward to making conver-
sation with her, but I couldn't face explaining the complex matter of returning Willie's present, and, in any case, I didn't want
to embarrass him by talking to his mother about it, and I didn't
want to leave it with no explanation at all. I was beginning to
feel uncomfortable about insisting that Leah give the thing back.
How was he supposed to have known better? His moth[...]
couldn't manage to answer the doorbell by herself, and w[...]

one had done it for h...
w to say something a...ing to talk to her about. A stack
...ter," or "Won't you...ffee table, but the one on top of the
I looked around f...oor Life, and it felt like a tactless choice.
of magazines sat ...
pile was an issu...dress was the kind I associate with the
Her flowere...McCarthy-era films about what to do when the
women in ...p the bomb. I guess we could've debated the pros
Russians ...
and ...ns of duck and cover, but we didn't because I noticed
the one ...zable nonaquamarine object in the room, a large,
fram...d family tree that hung over the fireplace.

"Your family." I smiled and gestured toward it. It was the most familiar-looking thing in the room. Anyone interested in purebred dogs is, of course, expert at reading pedigrees, and genealogical diagrams of human lineage are simple and straightforward compared with the ones that trace canine ancestry. For a start, in human family trees, the same individual tends to appear only once, but in a linebred dog's pedigree, the same names show up more than once, and if there's been close inbreeding, the trunks and branches of the family tree twist in and around each other in a scandalous tangle.

"Johnsons and Smiths." Her voice was a little hollow, but less than it had been. "Smith was my maiden name."

"Oh," I said brightly.

"And Johnson is a very old name, too," she added proudly. I gave her a vacuous smile, and she went on. "And one of my ancestors was a cousin to President Zachary Taylor."

"Oh," I said again, unimpressed. A mere cousin? Why, Rowdy and Kimi are *direct* descendants of Ch. Gripp of Yukon. But I didn't tell Edna. It might have made her feel inferior.

"And on Mitchell's side, the Johnson side, there's a Clark and a French." Her face had brightened up, and her little eyes changed from flat to beady. "And, of course, his mother was a Dale, and his grandmother was a Mitchell."

In lieu of saying something—what?—I got up and took a look at the framed diagram. Like Rowdy's and Kimi's pedigrees, it consisted mainly of precisely arrayed names, but neither of their pedigrees has a tree sketched around it, and the lines aren't embellished with tiny oak leaves. Anyway, I didn't have trouble ...iphering the two most recent generations in the Johnson-

Smith pedigree: Mitchell Dale Johnson had m........
abeth Smith, and they'd produced three sons. T......
William Smith Johnson, and—I swear I am no......
up—both of the others were named Mitchell Dale......
Yes, both. The American Kennel Club, for God's s...........
let you register two dogs under the same name. Who...otects
children?

"What did you say your name was?" Edna sounded as if I
might not have one.

"Holly Winter," I said.

"Winter," she repeated suspiciously.

"Winter."

Rufous Winter fought in the American Revolution. Consequently, I'm eligible for the DAR, but damned if I'll ever join,
and damned if I'd tell Edna Johnson, particularly because I
knew what she was going to ask me next, and I had the perfect
answer all ready. My mother coached me on it. Edna was about
to ask, "Oh, and what kind of name is *that*?" Marissa taught
me to smile politely and answer: "A kennel name."

But I didn't have the chance. Willie rushed into the room,
slammed to a halt, and looked first at me and then at the brown
paper bag on the floor near my feet. "Ma, your stuff's in the
kitchen," he told Edna, who obediently scurried off. He looked
at me and said, "Yeah?"

"Willie, Leah is only sixteen," I said. "She hardly knows you.
This is really a generous present, but, um, it's a little too much.
I just can't let her take it."

He put on the same look he'd had when he told Jack that
he was sorry about Rose, stiff and apologetic, but this time, I
realized that whatever manners he'd learned he'd got from TV
or the movies and that he wasn't surprised to find that he'd got
something wrong.

"I know it's really a good, uh, one," I said with that stupid
adult fear of using a dated word to someone not all that much
younger. "And you're welcome to come and visit, or whatever.
It was really generous of you. It was nice of you."

Preoccupied as I was with my own prissy insensitivity and
the look of stolid, repeated hurt on Willie's face, I didn't hear
either Edna or Dale, but when I'd assumed that she'd gone to
the kitchen to unpack the groceries, she'd evidently gone in
search of Dale. They stood in the front hall looking at us, the

other half hidden behind the oafish son. Edna looked confused and frightened. Although she never left the house, her face said that, even so, she felt a terrifying uncertainty about where she was and, probably, who she was and who these other androids were.

Dale, though, understood. "My brother's not good enough?" He puffed himself up and folded his arms across his chest.

"You probably just heard me telling him we'd be glad to see him," I said.

"You know how much he paid for that?" Dale demanded.

"A lot," I said.

He proceeded to tell me how much. He also told me how hard his little brother worked and how much overtime he put in. I was pretty sure that at the fun match from which he'd been evicted, he'd been too far away from me to notice or remember me, but it was clear that he'd at least connected Leah, dog training, and me, because he started making the same accusation Leah had made earlier, that I was a snob, and went on to damn everyone else who trained dogs, too. His little brother was good enough for anyone, he said. Then I thought I heard him say that Leah and I were both Japanese, but a second later I decoded the acronym. JAPs, he'd called us, Jewish-American princesses.

A happy look of comforting recognition crossed the empty perplexity of Edna's face, and she finally asked the big question that Willie's arrival had cut off: "What kind of a name *is* 'Winter,' anyway?"

Before I'd decided whether to let her think it was Jewish or to tell her the canine truth, Willie, who'd been cringing in silence, said sharply, "Mom, enough."

"Willie, shut up and stay the hell out of this," Dale growled at him. He turned on his brother just as fiercely as, seconds before, he'd defended him.

Although Dale hadn't actually threatened me, I'd imagined that if I tried to cross the hall and reach the front door, he might block my way. Maybe it was cowardly and opportunistic to take advantage of his rapid switch to targeting Willie, but I did. Never step into a same-sex dog fight. You'll only get bitten.

"Willie, I'm sorry," I said lamely.

I brushed past Dale and the pathetically cowering Edna. As I undid a dead bolt and pulled open the front door, I heard Dale laughing at Willie. Then, of all things, Dale started singing an old Beatles song. His voice wasn't bad. The effect was freakish and weirdly poignant, partly because he was right. You can't buy love.

Chapter 12

"So is that sick or what?" I said to Rita, who was curled up on her couch with Groucho, her rapidly aging dachshund, on her lap.

Leah, Ian, Seth, Miriam, a mollified Jeff, and four or five of Leah's other best friends had taken over my place to study the immortal James Dean (double feature: *Rebel Without a Cause, East of Eden*) on Rita's VCR. She and I were drinking gin on the rocks in her maturely furnished and frigidly air-conditioned living room, which is a floor and a cut above mine.

I went on telling Rita about the Johnsons. "The same names! Three Mitchell Dale Johnsons! I mean, people think that, in a way, *my* family is sort of eccentric. And I was embarrassed, once I got old enough to really understand that if you heard 'Holly Winter,' especially if you heard my middle name, you'd assume I was a dog. What else could you think?"

When Rita took a sip of her gin, the gold bracelets on her wrist clanked, and Groucho's eyes opened. "What is your middle name?" she asked. "I don't think I've ever heard it."

"Good," I said. "Anyway, I went through a phase of being ashamed of having a name that sounded like a dog's, but that isn't half as bad as having exactly the same name as everyone else. So why would anyone do that? I mean, why name your first two kids after yourself? And the only rational explanation is that the guy Mitchell, Senior, was really determined to have a son named after him, and he did it twice in case one of them died. And the first didn't, or at least he hasn't yet. So wouldn't the second one feel like sort of a spare part? Wouldn't he end up saying to himself, Well, they had me in case the first one got broken? But since the first one didn't, they're probably thinking

79

that they're sorry they wasted their time and money on me. Sick, right?"

"It depends." The more gin Rita drinks, the more everything depends. "Narcissistic. But pathological?"

"Come on. How would you like it?"

"You think I'm kidding? It does depend. Sometimes it's clearly pathological. I once saw a family where the mother, the daughter, and the dog were all named Alice." When a therapist says she saw a family, she doesn't mean that she just looked at them. "Fact. Alice. All three."

"Oh," I said. "What kind of a dog was it?"

"Holly, really. The point is, it was a dog. As a matter of fact, it was a cocker spaniel."

"Oh."

"What does it matter?"

"Some breeds are more sensitive than others," I said authoritatively. "So what happened to the three Alices?"

"You don't want to know." She looked down at Groucho and patted his head. I hoped she couldn't see how frail he'd become.

"Yes, I do," I corrected her. "How come they ended up with you?"

"They put the dog to sleep, and the daughter got the message. What happened was that one day she got home from school, and the dog wasn't there, and they told her they'd taken it to the vet and had it put to sleep."

"They murdered a dog named after . . . ? Jesus. So what happened?"

"So the daughter became more and more reclusive, developed a severe school phobia. And, naturally, insomnia. 'Put to sleep' was the parents' phrase. And she had a psychotic episode. The business with the names and the dog wasn't their only problem, of course."

"Names aren't the Johnsons' only problem, either. Another is what I was telling you before, that the house is like some dirty aquarium. Anyway, another thing is that Edna never leaves home. She has whatever that phobia is."

"Agoraphobia?"

"Yes."

"And how old are the kids?"

"They aren't. Willie is eighteen or so, I think, and Dale— that's the second Junior—is older. The birth dates were on the family tree. Dale is maybe twenty or twenty-one. And the oldest one is somewhere around twenty-five."

"They all live at home?"

"You know, you really have a prejudice about that. There are lots of perfectly nice, ordinary families where that's normal."

"Sometimes it is," Rita said. "It depends."

"Jesus."

"I'm serious. It depends on whether they *don't* leave or they *can't*. There's a big difference."

"Well, I hope Willie can. And does. Although . . ."

"Although?"

"Although they both, Willie and Dale, they both treat her as if she's not all there, not *compos mentis,* which is true enough, if you ask me. I feel awful. I didn't mean to, but I really did make things worse for Willie. I shouldn't have done that."

People who don't have a therapist as a friend and tenant sometimes imagine that therapists are always telling everyone not to feel guilty about anything, but those people don't know Rita. "No, you shouldn't have," she said. Then she added, "But how were you to know?"

The next morning after I fed and walked the dogs and gave them some water, I took both of them back outside to the driveway and used a shedding tool, a wire slicker brush, a metal comb, and three or four hairbrushes to remove what I guessed was enough woolly undercoat to make one mitten or a narrow scarf. After that, starting in the kitchen, I vacuumed up the fur in every room except Leah's—she was still asleep—and finished by redoing the kitchen, because the baseboards and corners were already starting to fill up again. As I vacuumed, I thought about what would happen if you crossbred poodles, which don't shed, with malamutes. If you planned it right, you see, you'd get the ultimate perfect dog, the French-Alaskan poolamute: a non-shedding, weight-pulling sled dog of wolflike appearance that would become an Obedience Trial Champion and say *woo-woo* instead of *ruff-ruff.* But will the American Kennel Club recognize the breed?

When Leah finally got up, I said to her, "Hey, since you've basically taken over Kimi's training, and since they're both really starting to shed, I wonder if maybe you could take over grooming her? I mean, since she's more or less your dog for the summer."

"Sure," Leah said, and with a mock-Spanish accent added, "No pro-blem," exactly what Jeff, Ian, Emma, Noah, and all of the others kept saying and exactly how they kept saying it.

"And help with the vacuuming?"

"No pro-blem."

"Good. Kimi's been out and fed, so don't let her convince you she hasn't had breakfast, because she has. I want to do an article about Rose, a memorial thing, and probably it's not national enough for *Dog's Life,* but one of the local ones might take it, and I just feel like doing it. Anyway, I need to go look something up, and then I'll be back."

The famous person-obedience academy down the street from me has the largest university library system in the world, but its canine collection is limited. That's okay. Although the AKC library is inconveniently located in New York City, the Stanton Memorial is right on my own Appleton Street, and dogs are allowed. By the time Rowdy and I crossed Huron Avenue, the heat was getting to Rowdy, and at the Stanton he sprawled on his side and slept under the long oak table in the reference room while I looked up the old stats on top obedience dogs and top obedience poodles. Rose Engleman's last poodle, Vera, had just under a thousand lifetime points, and in the last year she was listed, about a hundred more than Heather Ross's last poodle. On the other hand, Panache, the poodle Heather had now, was in the top twenty-five by points earned last year, and Caprice wasn't, maybe because she was younger than Panache, and also because Heather hit a lot more trials than Rose did. In the Delaney System, which recognizes only the dogs that place first through fourth in an obedience class and in which the dog gets one point for every dog it defeats in its class and . . . Well, never mind. Anyway, over the years, in the Delaney System, Rose and Heather looked close enough so that if I'd been as competitive as Heather, I'd have felt relieved to know that statistics for next year would show Panache a comfortable few hundred points ahead of Caprice, if not a lot more.

I also chanced to notice that the top dog in the Delaney System, O.T.Ch. Shoreland's Big Harry Deal—a golden, what else?—had 5,042 points, whereas the highest ranked Alaskan malamute, Northeast's Tahkela Amarok, C.D., had 44. So,

5,042 points? Would I kill for that? Would I kill for 44? Well, no. Malamutes are malamutes, and nobody would kill for 44 points. But poodles aren't malamutes, and the top poodle had 3,456 points and came in third in the Delaney ratings, and I couldn't help thinking that although I wouldn't actually murder someone for 3,456 points and third place, I might be slightly tempted to do some harm. And if I might, what about Heather?

Chapter 13

MALAMUTES believe that summer is your fault. On the ninety-plus-degree sidewalk outside the library, Rowdy glared at me and pulled his statue-of-Balto act. I had to make him heel to get him to move at all, but when I released him on my block of Appleton, a few houses from home, he bolted to the back steps, flew up them, and then eyed me impatiently while I unlocked the door. When I did, I knew right away that Leah had gone out: The phone was ringing. Whatever other household tasks people her age may fail to perform, one they never, ever neglect is answering the phone.

I picked up in the kitchen, held the receiver to my ear, and with my free hand, turned on the cold water tap, filled Rowdy's bowl, and lowered it to the floor.

"Holly?" The female voice was familiar.

I said yes.

"Lisa Donovan. From dog training? 'Member I said I'd talk to my neighbor? The one that weaves?"

"Sure."

"Well, she's interested. Her name's Marcia Brawley." When she'd spelled it for me and given me a phone number, we spent forty-five minutes talking about dogs and trading information about upcoming shows, obedience judges, and show sites. We weren't just gossiping. It's a waste of time and money to enter a dog if the obedience rings are jammed together next to the dumpsters on a broken-asphalt surface and the judge hasn't read the AKC regulations for ten years because he knows what he likes.

As soon as I got off the phone with Lisa, I called Marcia Brawley. I'll admit that by that time, I was hoping she wouldn't want to talk about dogs, but she did. She was feeling guilty because a border collie needs to work, and she was afraid that hers, Rascal, was becoming neurotic because he lacked a sense of purpose. What did I think about getting him a pair of sheep so he'd have something to herd? And, of course, she could use the wool, speaking of which, was it a scarf I had in mind? And did I want pure malamute wool or sheep blend?

"Oh, pure," I said. Just the idea of the blend put me off, mostly, I suppose, because it suggested crossing a malamute and a sheep, in other words, a nightmare: the strongest, stupidest animal on earth, and given the predator-prey conflict inherent in its hybrid genes, one that would probably go for its own throat. "Unless there's some reason . . . ?"

"Not really. It's a matter of what you like. You want to look at some samples? I've got a nice Akita wall hanging, but they're picking it up tonight, so if you want to see it, it'd better be today."

The Brawleys' big mauve Dutch Colonial was on the street across from the park, and the sun-room that ran along one side of the house was Marcia's studio. A loom about the size of a baby grand piano sat at one end, and except for the two chairs in which we were sitting and the worktable between us, the remaining contents consisted almost exclusively of natural fibers. Underfoot was a rough-woven woolen rug in the colors of Joseph's coat. Hand-loomed curtains kept out the sun. Neatly arrayed along all nonglass wall surfaces were spools, bobbins, and rolls of yarn and thread, most in natural shades of brown, gray, and off-off-white, but a few in loden, berry, and heather.

I'm so used to Cambridge that I seldom notice the absence of makeup—you're deported to the suburbs if you're caught with blue eye shadow—but Marcia Brawley's invisible lashes were more emphatic than any mascara, and her Scandinavian hair accented her sun-damaged skin.

She'd carefully wrapped the Akita hanging in tissue and was now spreading out a long, wide muffler woven in six or eight different shades of brown. "What about something like this? Only not this color, of course. Unless you want it dyed. You don't want it dyed, do you? You want it natural."

"I think he'd like that better," I said. I pulled a tightly sealed plastic bag from my purse and handed it to her. "This is just what's coming out now. My dogs both have white undercoats.

Kimi has some tan, but not much. But once they start losing the guard coat, it'll be gray—some dark, some light—and black, and more white . . ."

"Of course." She opened the bag and, like a baby rubbing a blanket ribbon, ran the fur between her fingers.

"Look, I don't know anything about weaving," I said. "Is it all right? Can you do something with it?"

"Of course."

I was happy that my fur—well, Rowdy's and Kimi's—had passed inspection. We discussed the dimensions and design of the scarf and settled on a price that seemed reasonable enough, especially if you consider that the raw material was going to arrive really raw, fresh off the dogs.

Finally, since a profile of a weaver who'll card and spin what your pet sheds is exactly the kind of piece that *Dog's Life* will always buy, I asked Marcia how she'd feel about an article. She was flattered, even though *Dog's Life* isn't exactly *The New Yorker*. The big difference is that *New Yorker* profiles focus on people, whereas the *Dog's Life* reader wants mainly to read about dogs. As you can imagine, then, I hoped that Rascal, her border collie, was photogenic and personable. I hadn't even met him. I asked where he was.

"He was with Zeke," she said, going to the window and pulling open one of the curtains. "My son. Maybe they're back. Yeah, there's Rascal."

"Your yard's fenced?" Newton has a tough, enforced leash law. I assumed that the dog wasn't wandering loose. Marcia didn't say anything, and I went on. "I love Cambridge, but most of the yards are so small. I always feel guilty about my dogs when I see one with lots of room."

"Yeah. Actually, we used to live in Cambridge. Before." In Newton, that means B.C.: Before Children. "We moved here for the schools. Just like everyone else." She looked apologetic. "We've been here, um—Zeke was four, so it's five years. You get used to it."

"I'll bet," I said as Marcia walked me to the door. "And a big fenced yard for your dog. That must be more than a little compensation. I mean, if you've got enough room so you can even think about having sheep, too. Nice."

Just as Marcia opened the front door, her telephone rang.

"Sorry," she said. "I've got to get that."

"It's okay," I said. "I'll call you about the article."

The first thing I did when I stepped outside was to look around for the fence so I could peer over it or open the gate to see what the dog looked like and say hello to him. As I was crossing the lawn, though, a rather small, mostly black male border collie with a lowered head dashed around a corner of the house, stopped abruptly, and stared at me. Maybe you've never been held in the gaze of a border collie. Have you ever been hypnotized, entranced, overtaken, and fixed in place? Same thing. I wasn't sure how to read this guy. He wasn't barking at me, but I was pretty sure he didn't want me to approach him, either. Well, I guess that says it: The effect of a border collie is to make you ask yourself what he wants you to do. They're small dogs, at least in the eyes of someone with malamutes, and they're fine-boned and fantastically agile, not burly or tough-looking, but they have an air of intense, authoritative intelligence. Goldens are the top obedience dogs in terms of raw numbers of titles, but there are lots of goldens and few border collies. If you take the numbers of dogs into account, the border collie is the unequaled, unbeatable great obedience breed.

I wondered whether I was supposed to say something, but this border collie, unlike the others I'd known, didn't issue the usual clear directions. Did he want me out of his yard? And what was he doing loose? Well, damn it, I thought. I should've known. He's so perfectly trained that they don't keep him tied up or fenced in. On the other hand, hadn't she said that he was neurotic? Or getting neurotic? I didn't return the stare, but I watched him out of the corner of my eye and began to edge my way toward the street. He maintained a steady three-yard distance from me until I reached the sidewalk, where he came to a peculiar, rapid halt, backed up, and barked.

A boy with Marcia's fair coloring came running around the side of the house and told him to quit it. He did. "He doesn't bite," the kid assured me. "And he doesn't go out of the yard."

"Ever?" I asked. "That's amazing. Border collies are such smart dogs. Did you train him?"

The kid shook his head no.

"But he's your dog? You're Zeke?"

He nodded.

"My name is Holly Winter. I've just been visiting your mother. She's going to make a scarf for me. A present for my father. Are you ever lucky to have a border collie! They're great dogs."

He smiled and patted Rascal's head.

"You go to school here, right? I forget the name of it. The one around the corner."

"Case," he said.

"Case. Did you have Mrs. Engleman?"

"Yeah," he said. "She died."

"I know," I said. "She was a friend of mine."

"She was a friend of mine, too."

It seemed like a strange thing for a boy of nine or ten to say about his kindergarten teacher. He reminded me of Rascal. They were both hard to read.

"I miss her," I said.

"Yeah," he said, taking the dog by the collar. "I gotta go."

"Me, too," I said. "Bye."

I didn't notice the collar until Zeke wrapped his hand around it. I still didn't understand Zeke, but I knew why Rascal didn't move beyond the lawn, why no ugly chain link marred the pretty landscape. Here's how it works. Around the perimeter of the yard, you bury a wire that transmits a radio signal that's picked up by a receiver on the dog's collar. Whenever the dog crosses the boundary, he hears a warning beep. Warning? Oh, yeah. If he doesn't back up instantly, the collar gives him an electric shock. A system like that isn't cheap, but, as I've said, it doesn't mar the pretty landscape.

Chapter 14

As soon as I got home, I kicked Leah, Jeff, and some of the Seths and Emmas out of the kitchen, sat down at the table, buried my toes under Rowdy's nonelectrified chin, and did a column about electronic training. My editor, Bonnie, had rejected my previous columns and articles on the topic because the subject "is not of interest to the readers of *Dog's Life.*" The readers she had in mind were mostly advertisers, not subscribers, but she's right that some of our readers do use electronic trainers and might not be happy to read that they ought to quit. As I told Bonnie after the last rejection, St. Paul's editor probably told him that the Epistles were not of interest to the Corinthians, either. Bonnie replied rather sharply that I'm hired to write about dogs, not to spread the gospel. Then she hung up. I felt angry and perplexed. I mean, I wasn't trying to suggest anything weird or radical.

Anyway, the column wrote itself, and when it was done, I outlined another on tips for removing dog hair from carpeting and upholstery.

"So probably I won't even bother mailing it," I told Rita, who stopped in when she got home from work. "And Bonnie'll love Holly's Household Hints, and she won't be mad at me, and I'll spend the rest of my life telling people how to get woven-in dog hairs out of the furniture. Christ! Here I am feeling like St. Paul, and I end up Heloise. Honest to God, I feel ashamed of myself. Just what you want to hear now, right? It's probably the first time today that anyone said that to you. I'm sorry. Scotch or gin?"

"Gin," she said, "if you have limes."

Because Groucho has never won anything at a fun match or

an obedience trial—he's never so much as been to one pre-Novice class—Rita has to buy serving trays, pottery sets, goblets, mugs, mint dishes, fruit bowls, candle holders, and compotes. Her tumblers and shot glasses are not engraved with pictures of hurdles and names of kennel clubs. Even so, she manages to contain her envy if I pour generously and refrain from reminding her that I could set a banquet table with the booty my dogs and my mother's have brought home over the years. When I'd dropped in ice cubes and lime, I added enough gin to clear the high jump.

"So how many patients did you see today?" I handed her the glass.

"Clients," she corrected me. "Eight."

"So what's one more? Because I have this feeling sometimes that I'm being driven crazy."

"So does everyone else," she said, "except the people who are."

"Would you mind listening?"

"I can't. I cannot listen. I am listened out. So talk, anyway. Just don't expect a response."

"Just one thing," I said. "When I feel like this? You know what I feel like? I'm in ancient Rome. Okay? And everybody says, 'Hey, it's been a stressful week, so let's go down to the Coliseum and have a few beers and watch the lions maul a few Christians.' Right? Well, there must've been a few people—there must've been a *few,* at least, mostly women, I bet—who said, 'But I don't *want* to. I think it's cruel.' So people said, 'What's wrong with you?' Here is this thing that is obviously cruel, and sometimes I feel like the only person who wants to yell, 'This is barbaric!' "

"You're yelling it right now," Rita said.

"Yeah, and at you. You see? It's pointless. You don't need to hear it. And what else do I do? I sit down and write a column that says that shock collars are great, and here's a whole new way to use them. You take the collar and put it around your own neck. Every time the dog does something you don't like, you push the button. Okay? Fair is fair. Who taught him to do whatever he did? Obviously, you did, so you're the one who gets jolted. I could probably think up a vicious name for my remote training method and market it. Maybe Marcia Brawley would buy that. I could make it really expensive. Marcia Brawley is this woman . . . She's a perfectly nice woman except that she gives electric shocks to her dog. Otherwise, she's a nice, civilized person. When in Rome. It makes me feel crazy."

Rita looked sad and shook her head. Then she drank some gin and licked her lips. "None of this is new to you," she said. "That there's a lot of cruelty? This is not new. And most of the time, you can step back and say, 'Well, why would someone do this? And how can I help her find a better way to get what she wants?' But today you write this adolescent essay about people putting shock collars on themselves. And you regress into this semi-grandiose vision, where the rest of us are sort of casual, decadent sadists and you're the only sensitive person on the planet."

"Grandiose," I said. I was glad I hadn't mentioned St. Paul. Rita is really amazing. She can spend all day with her patients or clients or whatever she's calling them at the moment and then still find the right words and, not only that, say them so you can hear them. "Yeah."

"You ever use a choke collar?"

"Yes. Everyone does, practically."

"Is it cruel? Does it seem that way to people?"

"Okay! Yes. The more I train, the less I use the training collar, and the more I use rewards. Okay. But I get the point: Judge not. If I have to correct a dog, I do, and there are people who'd say I'm cruel. And for all I know, the damned collar was her husband's idea. Maybe she objected, and they had a fight, and she lost. So now she feels ashamed. Probably she hates it. Or she doesn't know what else to do. Probably she's doing the best she can."

"Most people are," Rita said.

Among the people doing the best they could was Jack Engleman, who called me the next morning to ask me to stop in because he wanted some advice. I am not St. Paul, and there are a lot of kind people out there besides me. And, oh, yes. I am not always kind. But the fact is that Jack wanted my advice about yet one more act of cruelty in this kind world that is not—I repeat, not—ancient Rome. The cruelty was not, of course, Jack's and certainly not directed at Caprice, who was dancing and bouncing around as we sat at Jack's kitchen table drinking good coffee with real cream.

"Caprice looks good," I said. "You haven't let her put on weight." I'd been wondering whether Caprice was the reason he wanted to see me. It seemed hard to believe that she'd developed some kind of behavior problem, but dogs feel loss, too, and maybe she was showing it.

"She's fine, except she keeps bringing me her leash. Rose taught her to fetch it. Vera did the same thing. Rose'd say, 'Come on, let's do some work!' and Caprice'd go and get the leash and carry it to her. And now she'll just go get it, all on her own, and jump around all excited and look at me." He shrugged. "And I'm supposed to know what to do? I'm supposed to know where to begin? So I take it, and I tell her 'Good girl,' and maybe I take her out for a walk or I get her to dance or roll over or something, and then I give her a cookie, but she knows. She knows."

Cookie, by the way, is what a lot of old-time handlers call a dog biscuit. Don't ask me why, but they do, and the word reminded me of Rose, who always used it. My mother did, too. I hoped Jack also knew the right kind of cookies to buy, not those mushy supermarket ones, but the expensive, really hard ones that remove tartar.

"Jack, I know everyone must be saying, 'If there's anything I can do . . .' But is there?" It occurred to me that he might ask me to work with Caprice, to train her and handle her, or, preferably, from my point of view, to help him find a professional to do it. "Do you need any help with Caprice?"

He shook his head slowly and smiled. "Thank you," he said. "She's no trouble. The only trouble is she's still looking for Rose. And Heather Ross offered. She offered to handle her. But I don't think Rose would've liked that."

"I don't think so, either," I said, and then tried to make it clear that, unlike Heather, I wasn't fishing for a chance to handle Caprice. "I didn't mean . . . I mean, if you decide you want someone to handle her, I can find you someone, but I'm not a professional handler."

"Oh, no, no, I wasn't asking," he assured me. "No, no. Maybe sometime, but . . . No. What I want is . . . From time to time, you do some rescue work?"

Caprice gave a sudden bound and landed in Jack's lap. He rubbed the black curls on her head. I stared at both of them. It had never occurred to me that he'd want to get rid of her.

I must have looked horrified, but I nodded. "A little. Hardly any. Mostly a few malamutes. You want . . . ? But you don't need . . ." If he didn't want Caprice, he could sell her. The poodle rescue league, like all the others—for Akitas, goldens, malamutes, Dobermans, shelties, you name it—ends up with some wonderful, perfectly trainable dogs, but nobody but nobody hands over a dog like Caprice to a rescue league.

But I'd misread Jack. It was the first time since Rose's death that I'd heard his rolling laugh. "You should see your face!"

It was probably red. "I couldn't imagine, but . . ."

Then he turned serious. "Let me show you something. Caprice, move." She hopped to the floor. He got up, opened a cabinet, pulled out a photo developer's envelope, and came back to the table. "Rose was the world's worst photographer," he said. "Every picture she ever took had a tree sticking out of someone's head, or people had their eyes closed, or it was out of focus. But take a look at this, anyway."

In the photograph he handed me, the only object in sharp focus was the tall Norway maple between his house and the Johnsons'. The man and the dog to the right of the tree and some distance behind it, in the Johnsons' yard, were too blurred to identify with any certainty. The man's hair was blond, but he was even more out of focus than the dog, probably because he'd been moving. The dog looked like a shepherd, but I couldn't tell for sure which one. The man could've been either of the sons I'd seen. He seemed to be hitting the dog with something, maybe a baseball bat, but even the action wasn't entirely clear.

"Rose took this," I said. "Did she say who it is? And which dog?"

Jack shook his head. "Never said a word."

"Why?"

"The why's the one thing I know," he said, patting his thigh to call Caprice. She ran toward him and leapt into his lap. "Good girl." Then he seemed to change the subject. "You want to know something about a good marriage? I'll tell you a secret. You want to find a good husband, you find somebody who'll always give you a good argument. Religion, politics, anything. Whatever else you do, Holly, if you want to stay married, you don't marry yourself. You have to agree to disagree. And maybe nobody likes it, and nobody understands why you did such a crazy thing, but forget it. *You* do."

I wasn't sure I understood, but I nodded, anyway.

"So about any kind of trouble—causing any kind of trouble, stirring things up—Rose and I did not always see eye-to-eye. I wanted peace. I still do."

"With the Johnsons."

"With the Johnsons. And now? This is my home." He stretched a hand in the direction of their house. "Theirs is theirs. I want to stay, I live with them. We coexist."

"So when Rose took the picture, she just did it, and she had it developed. And she didn't say anything to you."

He nodded. "But she did talk about . . . You remember that case? She followed that very closely."

"The man who was convicted."

Jack nodded again. Practically everyone in Massachusetts knew about the case. A guy had been convicted and sent to jail sometime the previous winter or early spring because a smart, caring neighbor didn't just run out screaming and yelling when the guy was beating his dog with a board, but carefully took a whole series of photographs. The neighbor's photographic evidence was crucial.

"So," I said, "she knew that pictures would do it, that if she got it on film, she could really get him. It's a little hard to tell in this picture, but why else would she've taken it? She saw whoever it is beating a dog, and she remembered the case. So she got the camera. This is the only one? The only picture?"

"She was a terrible photographer," he said affectionately.

"Yeah." It was impossible to disagree. I nearly asked him whether he'd been keeping an eye on the Johnsons' house and yard, but I stopped myself. He'd had other concerns. "Obviously, this isn't enough. I wonder if . . . At a match, not so long ago—Rose was there—the middle brother, Dale, showed up with his dog, and he started hitting him, right there. There was sort of a scene. But . . . from what I can tell, this looks . . . Is this still going on?"

He looked as if I'd taken a long time to grasp the point. "You're asking me? I'm asking you."

"You haven't seen . . . ?"

"No, I haven't seen. I want peace, but not peace at any price.

And Rose understood that. She wasn't keeping any secret from me. She was waiting. And now . . . ? You've seen these dogs?"

"I've seen Willie's dog quite a bit, mostly from a distance, though. He trains with us, but I'm not in the same class. I'm not positive I can tell, but Righteous—that's the dog—he doesn't look abused. Usually you expect something. If you move your hand toward the dog, maybe he'll shy away. He'll cringe, or he'll show fear." I reached my hand across the table toward Caprice, who had planted herself cheerfully in Jack's lap. She elongated her neck and gave a happy little stretch in my direction. "That's exactly what you don't see," I said. "You can tell what she expects. Hands mean pats, food, good things. With an abused dog, you get the opposite. And they see feet, they expect to be kicked. But it isn't always that obvious. And those old stories about loyalty to abusive owners are basically true. You might think they'd hate the owners, but they don't. You're more apt to see fear. Or aggression. Sometimes it's real terror of something. A place. A situation."

"If it's going on . . ." Jack started to say.

"You have to decide," I finished for him.

He looked insulted. "If this is going on next door to *Rose's* house?"

"Of course," I said. "Look, about the pictures. Rose was right. That seems to be what works, lots of hard evidence. Pictures. Do you know how to use a camera? Could you . . . ?"

He didn't brag. All he did was show me some blowups of photos he'd taken of Rose, Vera, Caprice, and a couple of other poodles posed with a very young Rose.

"These are incredible," I said. I meant it. In case you didn't know, dogs aren't easy to photograph, and taking good pictures of dogs and people together is tough. "I guess you could more than manage a snapshot."

"I have the camera upstairs, loaded," he said. "By a window. Where Rose took this one. But I haven't . . ."

"There's the MSPCA. There's also a lawyer I know," I said. "He knows about things like this. If there's anything else you could do, or anything anyone can do, he'll know. You want his name?"

After I wrote it down for him, he walked me to the door. On the way, I told him that I'd been to see his sister and that she seemed like a terrific dentist.

"Charlotte's been a peach," he said. "The whole, uh, all of it, it's been easier since our mother passed away. Last winter, it was. She was, uh, she could never, never have accepted Rose."

"Has your father left? He's gone back to Florida?"

"Still with Charlotte." I had the grace not to say: "Oh, and not with you?" But the question must've shown on my face.

Jack leaned against the frame of the front door. "It's unbelievable. My mother passes away last winter, cancer. She's eighty-six, older than he is. You ask him, she dies of old age? No. Cancer? No. Her son married a shiksa. She died of a broken heart, he tells me. So now he's here, he discovers Charlotte's not keeping kosher. She hasn't kept kosher since she left for college, but now he discovers, and now she's a shiksa, and he won't eat here, it's all *trayf,* and he won't eat from Charlotte's kitchen, it's all *trayf,* too, all dirty."

"Isn't he getting hungry?"

"He eats deli. He eats nothing but deli, breakfast, lunch, dinner."

"It's probably very nutritious, anyway," I said.

"He has a lot to eat and a lot to complain about. He's never been happier." Jack beamed. "Eighty-five. Looks seventy. Acts fifteen. Myself, I want peace. Growing up in my family . . . they made the Knesset sound like a Quaker meeting. And now Don, my nephew, he says the word *autopsy.*" Actually, I was surprised to hear Jack say it. He was hardly Orthodox—Orthodox Jews don't believe in autopsies—and wouldn't object on religious grounds, but maybe I expected him to share my own family's taboo on uttering the word aloud. He went on: "Rose would care? I tell him, have I got news for you. Rose was not Jewish. Every year, in our home, she had a Christmas tree. But my father is ready to fight city hall, they did an autopsy on the wife of his son."

"He sounds very lively," I said.

"He leaves in forty-eight hours. Charlotte is counting them."

But I had the impression that if Jack's father liked complaining, Jack himself enjoyed complaining about the complaints. There was warmth in his voice when he spoke his sister's name and when he mentioned his nephew. Well, why not? He was happy to have his family back again.

Chapter 15

"THIS doesn't say anything about washing the dog," insisted Leah, waving a copy of the AKC Obedience Regulations. "All it says is that they can't be blind or deaf or 'changed by artificial means,' whatever that is. For all you know, soap is an artificial means."

All I knew was more than she did. "It means surgery and things like that. Bleaches. Dyes. It doesn't mean not to wash the dog." The rule doesn't ban training with shock collars, either, but it ought to. If an electric shock isn't an artificial means, I don't know what is. "Believe me, no judge wants to examine a dirty dog. At a minimum, you've got to brush her."

Rowdy was standing on the grooming table in the driveway. In preparation for a match the next day, I was religiously stroking his coat with a slicker brush. I'd started grooming him as soon as I returned from Jack's. Leah was sitting on the back steps with Kimi sprawled at her feet. Thick clumps of white undercoat grew like tumors from Kimi's flanks.

"But it's boring! Why don't we just wait until they're both done shedding and then clean it all up at once?"

"Because we live here, too, for one thing, and for another, I don't want to be seen with her looking like that."

"No one will care! And it's outdoors."

I gave in. "Okay. The agreement is that you're responsible for her. But don't blame me if the judge gives you a lecture about it, and he might."

"He probably won't even notice. I'm taking her to the Square, okay?"

"Fine. Good idea." One of the reasons I love Cambridge is that when you're training a dog, you want to work him in places that look, sound, and smell as much as possible like a dog show: Harvard Square, the human Westminster.

"And do you think I could use the car tonight? There's a party at Seth's."

Kevin Dennehy appeared on the sidewalk, overheard, and demanded: "Do his parents know about it?"

"Hi, Kevin," Leah answered, ignoring the question.

"Do they?"

"Kevin, relax," I said. "It's Newton. Would you let me worry about his parents?"

"I would if you would," he said.

"Yes, his parents know about it," Leah said. "They'll be there. See you later."

She and Kimi trotted away, and Kevin rushed off to meet some guys at the Y for a few hours of what Rita—but definitely not Kevin—calls male bonding. Leah and Kimi returned at five and left for Newton at seven, just as Steve and I took off for dinner with some friends of his in Watertown who have three rescue greyhounds. We tried to leave at eleven because Steve had to get back to check on a recuperating komondor, but it was hard to get away. When we did, Steve was worried about his patient. Because Appleton is a one-way street—you can't turn onto it from Concord Ave.—he dropped me on Concord opposite the front of my house instead of detouring around to reach my driveway and my back door, the one I always use.

I usually say that my house is on the corner of Appleton and Concord, but what's right on the corner, occupying a rectangular section of what would otherwise be part of my yard, is a long, very narrow, rather whimsical one-story structure known as a spite building and presumably built out of spite, revenge for some long-forgotten grievance. It's hard to imagine why else anyone would have built it. For a while, it was a sandalmaker's shop, but it doesn't look any more like a store than it looks like a house. In fact, especially because it has stood empty since the sandal shop closed, I didn't think of it as a building at all, but as walls that helped to enclose my property, an extension of my fence on which my dogs liked to lift their legs, thus prompting unliberated passersby to mistake Kimi for a male.

I crossed Concord and covered the narrow stretch of sidewalk that runs between the cars parked on Appleton and the spite building. Beyond the building, the sidewalk widens, and my own fence begins, but it didn't look like mine anymore. The fence is taller than I am, and so, I think, was the swastika spray-painted on it. The thing was about six feet by six feet, or maybe its obscenity and my rage made it feel bigger than it was. It jumped out at me, loomed over me, and swore wordlessly, but there were words there, too, sprayed on my fence, *my* fence: "Gas them all," I read, and "Jew lovers." I wanted to scream, cry, and belt someone—I actually did slam a foot hard against the fence—but I also felt a peculiar, irrational impulse to hide the thing: to rush to the cellar, grab a wide brush and a can of white paint, and blot it out before anyone else saw it. It was an urge to whitewash someone else's filth, filth directed at me, an impulse to cleanse myself.

A car passed by on Appleton, its lights illuminating the fence. I wondered who was in the car, whether anyone had seen the swastika, whether it had hit home. I couldn't paint it out until the police saw it, but I could call them, and I could screen it with something, throw something over it. Even so, Leah would have to know. I couldn't protect her from it, and when I wanted to wipe it out and be alone with my unquestioning dogs, she'd need to talk about it.

I could see from the driveway that the kitchen lights were on, and when I first walked in and caught sight of Leah, I thought that she'd not only discovered the thing but had felt so befouled by it that she'd taken a bath and washed her hair. Water was dripping from her curls onto the kitchen table, where she sat, and onto the adoring dogs whose chins she was rubbing.

"Damn, Leah. I hoped—"

But she interrupted me. "I am going to kill whoever did this! It is not funny. Practical jokes are not funny. They're just stupid."

I dumped my purse on the counter and sat down. "It doesn't seem like a practical joke to me," I said. "It feels a lot worse than that. It's not just some prank. You saw it when you drove up?"

"When I drove up? How stupid do you think I am? If I'd seen it when I drove up, I'd've known it was there, and I wouldn't't've got hit by it. I didn't notice it until it fell on me. I mean, I noticed the screen door wasn't shut right, but how was I supposed to—"

"Hold it. Start over."

"I drove in. I turned off the car. I got Kimi out of the back. Then I went up the stairs. The screen door was open a little, and I just thought, you know how it sticks sometimes? It doesn't shut all the way unless you pull it or push it. All I did was open it, and this bucket of water fell on my head. Is that stupid? You know what it is? It's juvenile."

"That's it?"

"Well, you know, it's not nothing. I just got wet, but the bucket could've hurt somebody, you know, if it'd landed hard on somebody's head. If it'd been you . . ."

"I hate to tell you," I said, "but it's not the only thing. I'll tell you about it."

"What is it?"

"I'll show you. But, first, uh, I've got to call the police, unless . . . You don't know if Kevin's home?"

She shook her head. "I didn't see him. Holly, did something really bad happen?"

"Yes," I said.

It was after midnight. Instead of knocking on Mrs. Dennehy's door or phoning there so late, I called the police. Maybe because I explained that I was Kevin's next-door neighbor and asked whether he happened to be there, a cruiser and two uniformed officers arrived pretty quickly, at least for Cambridge, which is not Newton, but not Boston, either.

One of the officers looked about fifty, the other about fifteen, but I could tell that the police-academy etiquette course they'd both taken hadn't changed over the years. I'm sure they both got A's, too, because they never addressed either Leah or me without calling us "Ma'am," and both displayed that mastery of facial expression that consists of showing none whatsoever.

Kevin Dennehy certainly didn't pull any higher than a C. Although he Ma'ams dutifully enough—not to me, of course, at least not anymore—his feelings register on his face and in his voice. That night, before he caught sight of Leah and me, he wasn't even making any effort to disguise them. He directed a muted bellow at his brethren: "What the hell is this all about?" Then he got closer and saw us and the dogs. "Sorry. Didn't see you. What the hell is going on here?"

We were on the sidewalk, and I pointed to the fence.

"Holy Christ," Kevin said. Then he read aloud: "Gas them all. Jew lovers." His solid, good voice felt like a husky, gloved hand that picked up the sprayed words and deposited them in a clear plastic evidence bag.

The child officer was shining a flashlight on the swastika. The color was primary red, not the barn red of my house, but it was close enough to gall me. I'd always liked the color of my house, exactly the shade my mother always used on the barn in Owls Head, and I didn't want anyone attaching bigoted, ugly associations to my house and Marissa's barn. Bigotry works like a permanent adhesive that glues the ugly to the innocent. During World War II, Americans started saying "Alsatians" instead of "German shepherds," but fools chased the dogs, tied cans to their tails, and persecuted them, anyway.

"Kevin," I said, kicking the bottom of the swastika, "I don't want this garbage on my fence. When can I paint it out? Can I do it now?"

"We have paint," Leah added. "I'll get it."

"No," Kevin told her. "Not yet. I'll let you know."

"Kevin, I am not having a goddamned swastika on my fence. I can cover it up. What if we hang some sheets over it? Nail them on or something."

He sighed. "Sure."

While he conferred with the guys in uniform, Leah and I took the dogs inside, where I dragged a white sheet out of a closet and, after some inspired ferreting in the cellar, brought up some odds and ends: plastic drop cloths, a hammer, a fistful of nails, two trim brushes, and an almost-full can of medium-blue paint left over from a chair I'd done a long time ago.

"Leah," I said. "Was Willie Johnson at the party tonight? Did you see him tonight?"

She shook her head.

"I didn't mention his name to those guys, but I have to tell Kevin. I haven't told him about that radio. The tape player. But he has to know."

"No!" she said. "That is not fair. You don't know."

"Leah, I have no intention of protecting whoever did this, and who else would? This was not some random thing. It was meant for us. Anyway, I'm not asking you. I'm telling you that I am telling Kevin the whole story. Look, in the meantime, I have an idea. Have you ever heard about something that happened when the Germans occupied Denmark?"

She shook her head. I could see that she was angry, but I went on.

"Well, they ordered all the Jews to wear armbands with Stars of David, and . . . Maybe I don't have the details right, but this is the idea. They gave the order, and the King of Denmark did a beautiful thing. He wore a Star of David, a Jewish star. He put on the armband, and then he went riding, or he went for a walk in a public park, or some other place like that, so everyone would see him."

"Like, 'Screw you,' " she said appreciatively.

"Yes," I said a little uncertainly. "Well, what I think he meant was, 'If you do this to anybody, you do it to me.' Or maybe, 'If you persecute anyone, you persecute everyone.' Anyway, we can't get rid of the swastika yet, but we can do more or less what he did."

We locked the dogs in my bedroom, spread a plastic drop cloth on the kitchen floor, and painted a defiant banner on a king-size sheet: a blue Star of David on a white background. It took us only a few minutes. When we carried it outside, Kevin and the other cops, who were still there, thought we were crazy. They wouldn't let us hang it over the graffiti—the blue paint was still wet—but I stood on a stepladder and nailed it to the top of the fence, *my* fence, so it hung next to the swastika. Leah probably thought I was crazy, too, but I felt wonderful. I am a Jew, the banner announced. I am Danish royalty.

Chapter 16

"AND tomorrow," I told Kevin, "I am adding ecumenical detail. A cross, unbroken. Pictures of Vishnu and Shiva. Anything else I can think of. Is there a symbol of Seventh-Day Adventism?"

Leah had gone to bed, the uniformed guys had departed, and Kevin and I were sitting on the back steps. He was sipping Budweiser. I was drinking milk.

"Hey, Kevin, what were you doing up, anyway? Did we wake you?"

"Nah, I was glued to the tube." He happens to suffer from insomnia, but whenever Rita calls it that, he gets furious. Last winter, when he went through a bad bout, she sat him down and delivered a serious lecture about stress management. In her version, she tried to get him to take a Zen meditation course. He reports that she tried to sell him to the Eastern brain-snatchers.

"So you were home?" I said. "Presumably, you were home when it happened."

"Yeah. Like I said. Now ask me again."

"Hey, there's no reason why you should've . . . I mean, you're not some patrolman assigned to this beat." That's one source of his insomnia. He grew up here, and he feels responsible for the entire neighborhood. "Anyway, there's some stuff you should know about this. And other stuff. And I have a match tomorrow, and I don't want to be wiped out, so I'm going to say it all fast, and I want you just to listen and not yell. First of all, you remember what happened in Newton, the graffiti, at the park, right? Well, in Leah's dog-training class there, there's a kid . . ."

I started to tell him about Willie, Dale, Edna, and the boom box, but before I even finished the part about returning the present, he interrupted me to say that the Newton police had already made the connection between the graffiti in the park and Willie's presence at the class, and hadn't he told me not to go there again?

"But Willie didn't necessarily do it," I said. "Either the other time or this thing. The whole family is, well, Rita would say that it's a dysfunctional family, I guess. And how come you know about them? Are you on some community liaison panel or something?"

"One," he said, "Saporski's mother still lives in Newton." As I may have mentioned, John Saporski is one of Kevin's best friends in the department. They used to play handball together at the Y, and they still go running sometimes. "And when this crap gets plastered all over a wall there, she expects him to do something about it. Two, M. D. Johnson and Sons is Cambridge."

"What?"

"It's in Cambridge."

"What is it?"

"Like the trucks say: disposable containers to the beverage industry."

"Which means?"

"Plastic cups," he said. "They're distributors. They distribute beverage containers."

"So you know about them from here? From Cambridge? How come? Do they distribute something else, too?"

He shook his head. "Nah. The problem was with the kids. Three of them, right? The old man, and three kids, and they all work for him. And when the oldest kid's maybe sixteen—old enough to drive—he starts hanging around the place after work, weekends. The place is down in East Cambridge, and it's a warehouse, and it's got offices, but it's got neighbors, too, and they start making complaints, and it turns out that when the place is closed, these kids are hanging around, drinking and shit."

"And they're underage."

"And then the neighbors get smart, and instead of calling us, they call the old man, and then instead of a bunch of kids, we get calls about domestic altercations."

"Between Mitchell Senior and the son? The oldest son?"

"By that time, it's two of them, the oldest one and this one you ran into, Dale, and they're a pair of prizewinners."

"So what was the, uh, domestic altercation? They were fighting with each other?"

"The basic scenario is that they hang around there, and they make a lot of noise and throw some bottles, and then the neighbors call the old man. And he shows up, and there's a lot more noise, and someone calls the station."

"And then there's heavy competition about who gets to go and intervene in a fight between a man and his two musclebound teenage sons. I'll bet that was a lot of fun."

"I just *love* domestic situations," Kevin said. "Wife calls because her old man's beating her up again, and when you get there and drag him off her, the next thing she does is grab a frying pan and bring it down on your head."

"So did anyone get hit with a frying pan?"

Kevin stuck out his lower lip and shook his head. "Cooled off now. The oldest kid shaped up. Went to some community college, and then he turned yuppie and drives around in a Corvette instead of a truck that says he sells plastic cups."

"So, you see? Willie wasn't really involved in that. Anyway, let me tell you the rest." I did. I finished with the blurred photograph Jack Engleman had shown me. "But they didn't know she took it," I said. "It was taken from inside. From the angle you could tell it was from an upstairs window. And she wouldn't have confronted them with it. Obviously, she'd been reading about that case—you remember—and what she wanted to do was accumulate evidence, pictures. Hey, you know what I wanted to ask you? Jack mentioned the autopsy. Do you know what it showed? I mean . . ."

"Pacemaker," he said.

"I know that."

"Yeah," he said. "And I heard . . . Saporski says it showed, uh, burns."

"From?"

Kevin shrugged.

"Right after Rose died, I asked Steve, because I had a sort of nightmare picture, like those scenes in the movies, of people in the electric chair. Anyway, I had this horrible image of her being burned to death. But he said that as far he knows, it doesn't do that, or not usually. Jesus. Was it . . . ?"

Kevin shook his head. "On her right hand. Two marks. Two burn marks on her right hand."

"From what? Look, I am so tired, but tomorrow or whenever, I have to tell you . . . It's basically about the pacemaker. First of all, these people who live across from the park swear that lightning didn't strike there, and so for a while I thought . . . The point is that pacemakers have something to do with radio signals, don't they? There's another house, right across from the park, where there's one of these electric fences to keep the dog in. Not the wire ones, you know, to keep cows in. The wire is buried. You can't see it. And basically, it works on radio waves. They're picked up by a gadget on the dog's collar. So I wondered if, somehow, that could've been . . . I mean, if lightning didn't strike, maybe what got to the pacemaker was something from that fence system, a radio signal. Electric storms interfere with regular radio, right? You hear static and all that. So it occurred to me that if that fence thing malfunctioned or whatever, it might've interfered with the pacemaker. The signals that were supposed to go to the dog's collar somehow reached her pacemaker. But that wouldn't leave marks, obviously. I don't see how it could burn. Could it?"

But Kevin was more interested in protecting Leah than in explaining the marks on Rose's body. "Has this Johnson kid been after Leah today? He been calling?"

"I don't think so," I said. "I don't know."

"Well, tell her if he does, hang up. Look, Holly, we'll follow this up, but the God's honest truth is that maybe nothing'll turn up. Between me and you, a hell of a lot of the time, there's not a damn thing we can do. And tell her if he calls, hang up."

Chapter 17

ASIDE from some deep reflex yawning, I was okay the next morning and, in fact, got up early to walk the dogs before the day really heated up. Then I packed the car. A sanctioned obedience match stands midway between a fun match and a trial. Consequently, people drag along only the minimum equipment, about half the paraphernalia they take to shows. You see the usual folding chairs and coolers as well as some crates, cages, and crate dollies, but especially because an obedience match has no breed rings and no electric hookups, people don't bother with grooming tables, tack boxes, hair dryers, extension cords, and the rest. On the other hand, a hot-weather trial—and outdoor obedience rings are always, always located in the sun-blasted dead center of a steamy field—requires dog-cooling equipment that you never see at an indoor show. The ice-filled cooler in the back of the Bronco contained two large spray bottles and two gallons of water. I also packed sunscreen, sandwiches, and iced tea for us, extra water and drinking bowls, dog biscuits, old towels to wet down the dogs, and, for Kimi, a terry-cloth hot-weather garment aptly known as a Wet Blanket.

As it turned out, she didn't need it. The trial took place at a park on the far western stretches of the Charles River, before the pollution leaks in, and Leah, barefoot in rolled-up pants, took a lightly and inadequately groomed Kimi for a wade and swim amid the goldens, Labs, Newfies, and Chesapeake Bay retrievers that were dashing in after sticks, thundering out, and joyfully shaking themselves off over the driest and most fastidiously dressed of the spectators. Rowdy condescended to dampen his paws at the edge of the river, stuck his muzzle rapidly in and out, and retreated to the bank. That's his idea of

109

a swim. When I tried to swaddle him in wet terry, he yelped as if I'd swatted him, but while he was busy eyeing a pretty Afghan hound, I slid a dripping towel under him to soak his belly and thighs.

Like most of the other handlers, Leah and I had set up in the narrow band of shade cast by the hedge that ran along one side of the field. Tamara Ryan, with only one Westie, and Lisa Donovan, with her English cocker, were on folding chairs on one side of us, which made me a little uneasy. I am not a breedist myself, but mostly because of a rotten-tempered, untrained, pet shop cocker kept tethered outdoors a block from our house, Rowdy detested cockers, and, in spite of all his show experience, I wasn't sure that he could tell the difference between a cocker and an English cocker. I couldn't blame him. In the eyes of cocker fanciers, the breeds are highly distinct, but I'm not always sure myself. In any case, either because he'd mastered the subtle distinction or because he was too hot to care, Rowdy was ignoring Davy.

"So, did you work anything out with Marcia?" Lisa asked, running her spread fingers through the back of her blond Dutch-boy hair to ventilate the nape of her neck.

"Yeah," I said. "She's making a scarf for me. Actually, not for me. A Christmas present for my father."

"She does nice work," Lisa said. "Lovely person."

I nodded blankly. Lovely persons do not half electrocute their dogs, but I don't like to preach.

"And," Lisa went on, "she's one of these people who do everything. Plays the cello, sort of semiprofessional—she's in some chamber music group—and does aerobic dance, teaches Chinese cooking for Community Schools, does all this PTA stuff. Used to be president, she and her husband, Larry. Now she runs the fair, which is more work than anything else if you ask me. Anyway, she's one of these people who make you feel totally inadequate, except you're glad: If she's doing it, you don't have to."

PTA?

"Oh," I said. "She didn't mention all that. Mostly, we looked at her work and talked about the scarf. But I did meet Zeke, on my way out. He told me he went to Case. Rose was his kindergarten teacher."

Tamara joined in. "Rose was everyone's kindergarten

teacher, everyone who went to Case. There's only one kinder-garten. You know she left a scholarship?"

"Really?" Lisa said.

"It's for Newton North graduates who went to Case," Ta-mara said. "College scholarship. Didn't you see? It was in *The Tab* and *The Graphic.*"

"Jack didn't mention it," I said. "I saw him the other day. I guess he started it. It's funny he didn't say anything."

Tamara shook her head. "It was Rose. You can contribute—probably he will, obviously—but it was Rose. I mean, they never had any children." She lowered her voice. "And there was money there. From her parents. She was an only child, and when they died, she got a bundle. And what else did she have to do with it? He doesn't need it, he's a broker. The bulk of it must go to him, but he doesn't need it, so why not?"

"Where did you hear that?" Lisa said.

"My sister. Her husband's a broker. He knows Jack. Every-one knew about it."

"I didn't," Lisa said.

"Well, everyone else did."

I was so busy listening that I almost lost track of what was happening in the rings. Then I noticed the armband on the han-dler in Novice B. "Leah, you're next," I said. "Go and wait by the ring. Have you been watching the heeling pattern?"

"Yes, yes, yes," she said. "Relax. And don't come with me. Stay here."

"You know you can give an extra command," Heather chimed in from a folding chair. The sun was so strong that even Heather and Abbey, who usually stationed themselves practi-cally inside the ring, were in the shade with the rest of us. Heather had removed her shoes and was daubing neat rectan-gles of Panache-like silver-gray polish on the backs of the heels. "If she lags, tell her to heel. You know you can do that. You'll lose points, but don't let her get away with it."

Leah nodded politely, brought Kimi to heel, and trotted off confidently. Her hands weren't shaking, her knees weren't knocking, and her face hadn't turned the usual novice ashen green. As I watched her downshift to a stride, I noticed at the far edge of the field, in the shade of a maple grove, one handler warming up a dog, heeling him back and forth, drilling him on about-turns. The dog was Righteous. The handler was Willie

Johnson. I hoped he had the sense to keep Righteous away from the ring while Kimi was working. The sudden appearance of a dog at ringside is a powerful distraction. Willie wouldn't deliberately plant his shepherd there to ruin Kimi's performance—it's done, oh, is it ever—but he was a novice and might do it inadvertently.

"Doesn't she look like your mother?" Heather called to me. As I may have pointed out, everyone knew Marissa. "Have you noticed? She looks a lot like your mother, and she sounds like her, too. Or maybe you don't remember."

"I remember," I said. "I remember very well." Then I stopped talking. I didn't want the sound of my voice to distract Kimi.

With Leah and Kimi in the ring, I finally turned my attention to the center of the field, where the sun was broiling the dogs and handlers and had already begun to burn the judges and stewards. Not a single spectator stood near any of the roped-off rings, and the usual collection of folding chairs, dogs, and waiting exhibitors was absent, as if the sun had worked like a self-cleaning oven to bake them into an invisible powder.

Does the mental transmission of orders count as double handling? If so, I cheated. *Don't let her down,* I commanded Kimi. *Watch Leah. Sit. Sit straight. Heel! Sit! Stay, damn it! Don't you move. Don't you dare pull anything. Good girl! Beautiful work!*

Or maybe they did it on their own. Except at the end, when the ribbons are handed out, applause goes exclusively to very young junior handlers, real children, not people Leah's age, and to dog-handler teams that have done something spectacular. If you ask me, anyone who has the guts to walk into an obedience ring with an Alaskan malamute deserves a cheer—it's like wing-walking on an antique biplane with an unpredictable engine, a senseless act of courage—but sometimes all you get is kindly silence intended to convince you that no one was looking, anyway. That hot day, though, people were watching: Leah's hair flashed like a beacon, and the temptation to observe how creatively a malamute will fail to qualify is more than most people can resist. At the end of a perfect recall, the last individual Novice exercise, Kimi did a flawless finish, and when Leah released her, the applause was loud, even in the big, open field. Leah and Kimi pranced proudly back. I'm not sure which had the bigger grin or which of them I hugged harder.

"Leah, that was really beautiful," I said. "And in this heat? Beautiful. Look, I've got to exercise Rowdy and warm him up a little. Give her a treat, and don't let her drink too much water, just a little at a time, and then cool her off before the sits and downs. Drench her. It's brutal for them out in that sun, and on a day like this, even a perfect dog will break sometimes."

As it was, I did no more than catch their group exercises out of the corner of my eye, because Rowdy and I were busy in another ring, where the ninety-five degrees melted his usual inventiveness. When I sent him over the high jump, he soared, but I could feel him ponder the possibility of ambling slowly and coolly back around it. "Jump!" I yelled silently, and he sprang up nicely, clearing the top with room to spare, returned briskly, and sat only a trifle crooked to present the dumbbell.

Rowdy and I had only a short break before the group exercises, just enough time to get some water in, on, and under him and to learn that Kimi had qualified. As I returned to the ring at the end of the long down, I spotted a dark blotch in the shade under the judge's table, but it turned out to be someone else's blotch, a black standard poodle who'd decided it was better to be out of the sun than in the ribbons. Rowdy was impatiently twitching his plumy white tail back and forth, but he was where I'd left him, and unless he'd taken a stroll in my absence, he'd qualified.

Back in the shade, Leah was pouring water into Kimi's bowl.

"So?" I said.

"So we qualified." She sounded as if there'd never been any doubt, but the excitement showed on her face.

"Great!" I upended a water jug on top of my head, sent a cold stream down my back, took a big swig, and poured the rest into Rowdy's bowl. Then I rummaged in my kit bag for the dogs' rewards, outsize dog biscuits I reserve for shows. The dogs were nuzzling and salivating, but as I pulled out the biscuits, Kimi vanished, and Rowdy hit the end of his leash. When I looked up, Abbey was holding out two closed fists. Rowdy was bouncing and eyeing her hands, and Kimi, the furry piranha, was about to strike.

"Okay?" Abbey said. "Homemade microwave liver."

Heather and Panache were nowhere in sight.

"Sure," I said. "They've earned it. Thanks."

The dogs snatched the brown stuff from her hands and licked

her palms clean, but she scrubbed her hands with a towel, any-way.

"Sorry, guys," I said to the dogs as I gave them the biscuits. "Second best, but all I've got. Microwave, huh?"

Abbey nodded. "Works like magic."

"I do liver in the oven sometimes," I said, "but not in the summer. It takes forever, and you can't get rid of the smell."

"You ought to get a microwave," Abbey said. "You just throw it in and nuke it. We got it from Rose because she didn't trust it after she got the pacemaker. You knew about that?"

I nodded.

"Well, after she got it, the microwave made her nervous. I gather that if they don't work just so, they mess up the pace-maker. Hers was okay, but she wanted to get rid of it, anyway, and she gave it to us, and there's nothing wrong with it. You ought to get one."

"Obviously, the dogs think so," I said.

Soon afterward, Heather and Panache came dancing back on silver heels, and a couple of minutes later, the stewards started calling us back into the rings—that is, those whose dogs had qualified. A sweet-faced young woman and her Bernese moun-tain dog stood just in front of Rowdy and me at the head of the line along the edge of the ring. The Bernese mountain dog happens to be one of my favorite breeds. They're big, strong dogs with long, silky black coats and white and rust markings, gorgeous dogs and loving, loyal companions. This one was a very feminine-looking bitch, probably too small to show in breed, but a first-rate obedience worker. I'd seen her at other shows, and I'd watched her today.

"She's doing great," I said to her handler. "I saw her today."

"Yeah, she's finally shaping up," the woman said.

"She looks great. Did you have some . . . ?"

"Yeah, she started giving me a hard time, and I had to get out the old electronics. But that took care of that." She smiled and patted the dog's head. I wanted to kick her.

The Bernese mountain dog got first place, of course, but when the judge handed me the second-place ribbon and a drinking glass for the collection, Rowdy knew who'd really won. When people applauded, he woo-wooed, and as the judge kept handing out the ribbons, he kept it up, and some of the spectators started

laughing. The Bernese won first place and my sympathy, but
Rowdy won the crowd.

"Happy worker," commented the handler of the Bernese
mountain dog, meaning that Rowdy had never been serious
competition. "Congratulations."

"Thanks." I walked away. "She thinks I'm a sore loser," I
told Rowdy. "Let her."

Against some mean competition in Novice B—it looked like
a poodle breed ring—Kimi won third place, plus yet another
tumbler, and Leah underwent a rapid shift in apparent age from
a cool twenty-one to an ecstatic, unguarded twelve. "Isn't she
wonderful? Aren't you proud of her? She is the most wonderful
dog in the world, aren't you, Kimi? Aren't you? So now I can
register her for a trial, right? The second we get home."

As I finished packing up our belongings, the fatigue suddenly
hit me hard. "Speaking of home," I said, thinking disjointedly
of PTA presidents, pacemakers, microwaves, and the old electronics, "how would you like to drive? I'm sweltering, and I'm
so tired. Oh, there's Bess. You ought to tell her. Her feelings
will be hurt if you don't."

Near the registration table, Bess Stein was surrounded by
people and dogs, including, I noticed, Willie Johnson and
Righteous. The sides of Willie's head looked freshly shaved. He
had the dog's lead in one hand and a green qualifying ribbon
in the other.

"Hey, Willie," Leah said as happily as if our fence had been
washed in white instead of fouled in red. "Congratulations! Hi,
Righteous. You were a good boy, huh?"

In back of Willie stood a young man I had no trouble identify-
ing as the third Johnson brother—in other words, the first
Mitchell Dale Johnson, Jr. He had the same white-blond hair,
thick cheeks, and heavy-boned build as Dale and Willie, but he
was thinner than the other two, and his hair was slicked back
on the sides and poufed up on the crown of his head. He had
on tasseled leather loafers, tan pants with sharp, deliberate
creases, and an unfaded black polo shirt. My own white pants
were grass-stained and wrinkled, and I hadn't combed my hair
since I'd doused it with water, but I didn't feel inferior. I had
two Alaskan malamutes. The only animal he had was a small
embroidered horse over his heart, and someone else was riding
it.

"Nice husky," he said to me. About one person in a hundred gets it right. He pointed at Rowdy as if he were a flashy car, an object.

"Close," I said. "Alaskan malamute. Malamutes are bigger. They all have brown eyes."

"Tough, huh?"

I nodded. "Strong." Well, they *are* strong. "You Willie's brother?"

"Mitch." He extended his hand in one of those gestures that salesmen learn somewhere. When he shook my hand, I was aware that my palm was breaded in dog drool, IAMS biscuits, and fur, and that his wasn't, or it wasn't before. When he withdrew his hand, I could tell that he wanted to wipe it on something, but instead of scraping it off on his thigh, he reached toward Rowdy, who did something almost unprecedented. He braced himself on all fours and growled. I tried not to look stunned. The sound was very deep, almost inaudible, and deadly serious. "Don't touch me," it said. "And don't touch her again, either."

But Mitch heard it. "Sorry," he said, backing off a step. "Tough guy."

"He won't hurt you," I said. "But probably you shouldn't pat him, just in case. Rowdy, sit." He did, but he kept one eye on Mitch and the other on me. "Nice to meet you," I said to Mitch. "We've got to go. I have a fence to work on when I get home."

He looked puzzled.

"Someone painted it for me last night," I said, "but I don't like the color. It used to be white. Now it's red." Then I made a belated introduction: "I'm Holly Winter." I gestured toward Leah. Bess had an arm around her, and Willie was standing next to her. "That's my cousin, Leah. Well, nice to meet you."

It took me a few minutes to retrieve Leah and Kimi. Bess had to congratulate me and hear our score, and on the way to the parking lot, we ran into some people and spent a few minutes comparing notes and talking about the trials coming up. When we'd finally stashed the dogs and our gear in the back of the Bronco, I collapsed in the passenger seat, and Leah got the engine and the air-conditioning going. As she pulled out of the lot, I saw Willie cram his shepherd into the backseat of a red and white Corvette and lower himself in. Mitch, who'd been standing by the car giving people a chance to notice what he drove, climbed into the driver's seat and shut the door.

If people noticed the Corvette at all, what registered was probably nothing more than how out of place it looked among all of the full-size station wagons, vans, and roomy 4 × 4s bought to accommodate dogs, crates, grooming tables, coolers, and more dogs. The brothers looked out of place, too, and at a dog show or a match, that's not easy. Whether you're five or eighty-five, rich or poor, chunky or svelte, dressed in denim or velvet, the first thing people notice about you isn't you at all, but your dogs and how you treat them. After that? After that, I suppose it's a matter of looking at home, which doesn't necessarily mean having a dog with you, but does mean looking as if you should and, certainly, keeping your eyes on every dog in sight. Or maybe it just means looking happy. "Finally!" our faces say. "Finally! For once! For these few hours, enough fur! Bliss." In spite of the handsome shepherd and the green ribbon, Willie and Mitch didn't have that look. But I remembered where they'd come from.

Chapter 18

In the hours I slept after coming home from the match, a heavy rain fell, and cold, beautiful Canada delivered its most valuable export, a sudden temperature drop of about twenty degrees. In the late afternoon, Steve and I drove to Newton to let the dogs run in the woods that stretched behind and far beyond Eliot Park, the beer-lovers' lane that Rose and Jack had complained about. It wasn't a place I'd have gone alone at night even with two Akitas instead of two Alaskan welcome wagons, but in the late afternoon with Steve and his two dogs as well as Rowdy and Kimi along, the woods felt safe enough. Besides, they were wild-looking, with unpruned maples, oaks, evergreens, and underbrush. Any sensible dog owner realizes that in an unmaintained park like that, the narrow, rough trails may appear to meander and fork at random, but they don't. If viewed from on high, God's perspective, those paths spell out a hidden message: "Great place to violate leash law."

"The main thing," I was saying to Steve, "is that I don't trust kids at all. I at least understand dogs, but I don't understand children except that what I do understand is, if you try to housebreak them, it screws them up for life, and they chew things, and then they make a lot of noise, and then they leave. So if you want golden-haired babies all that badly, take Leah for the rest of the summer or get another dog. And could we talk about something else?" I snapped.

"PMS?"

"Shock collars."

"Radical remedy," said Steve, stopping to encircle my neck with his hands and making a loud zapping noise, "but it's not such a bad idea." Then he moved his hands and said softly,

"When you took that nap this afternoon, you could've called me. Just because you live alone, it doesn't mean you have to sleep alone."

"In case you've forgotten, I don't live alone until Labor Day. Leah and about five other kids were in the kitchen boning up for the SATs." I nuzzled my face in his once-navy T-shirt. Like everything he owns, it was faded and had a faint, lingering odor of chlorine bleach. A streak of adolescent self-consciousness makes him want to avoid smelling like dogs and cats. Actually, he smells like dogs, cats, and chlorine, but only if you're really close to him."

He ran his hands over my face and pulled my hair back, then started to kiss me, but Kimi and Rowdy came zipping down a wooded slope and landed at our feet. They squirmed around, tilted their big heads upward, widened their almond eyes, and began wooing. They weren't trying to protect me from Steve, of course. They just didn't want to be left out. When Steve's dogs—Lady, the pointer, and India, his perfect shepherd bitch—joined the circle, we gave up and resumed our walk.

"Actually, I do need to know about shock collars," I said. "You must hear about them, right? In veterinary school? Or you have clients who—?"

He shook his head. "Those people don't work with us. I probably don't know any more about shock collars than you do."

"You don't see burns? They do burn, don't they?"

"Oh, the old ones burned," he said sadly, kicking a small log off the path. "But not the new ones, at least not the expensive ones. Not unless they malfunction."

"But if they do? Or an old one. There ought to be two burns, right? I've seen the ads. And the catalogs. That's basically all I know, from that propaganda. Anyway, there are these plugs that go in the collar, with contact points, metal spikes. And that's what delivers the shock."

"Stimulation," he corrected sarcastically.

"Oh, right. Pardon the slip. Anyway, that's what would burn, right? The whole collar isn't electrified. It isn't a circle of electricity around the neck. It's two points, spikes, like bullets. They stick out of the inside of the collar and into the dog's neck. So if it burns, it'd leave two marks."

He shrugged.

"Steve, that's what they found on Rose's body. Two burn marks."

"On her neck?"

"No. Her hand."

"What would . . . ?"

"Well, that's what I'm asking you. But in theory, it's possible, right?" I pushed my way through some scrubby maple saplings.

"Hmm. She was opening the gate. She was found next to it. The marks could've come from the gate. It's galvanized. It's like a dog run. That's something we do see injuries from. The dog gets its paw caught in the chain link, that kind of thing. Has anyone taken a good look at the gate?"

"I assume. They must've. Anyway, we can look on the way out. But how would that burn? It isn't as if she'd scratched herself on it or got cut. Obviously, chain link could do that if it was loose. Torn. But Kevin said burns."

"If the whole thing was electrified? Say what's hit by lightning is a tree. Then the ground currents can radiate from the tree, or whatever's taken a direct hit."

"But the point is, there was no direct hit. There are these people who live across the street, right across the street from the entrance, where the tennis courts are. And they are positive. I talked to the woman. They were home. And they swear that lightning did not strike there. It's possible that it did and they didn't notice, but this woman sounds reliable."

"Then what . . . ?"

"That's it. What did? If lightning didn't strike, what was it? How did Rose die? I didn't see the autopsy report, obviously. Who's going to show it to me? But if her pacemaker had just sort of broken, if there'd been something wrong with it, there wouldn't be an inquest. Why inquire? Look, could it have been a shock collar? It'd leave two burn marks, and that's what she had, two burn marks. Could that do it? By the way, do you know where we are? I'm lost."

Four or five little paths led from the wooded clearing where we found ourselves.

He shook his head and took my hand. "No idea, but it doesn't matter. We'll just follow the dogs." My soulmate. "Anyway, could it burn? Yes. If it was old. If it was malfunctioning. Or if it'd been tampered with."

"Could you do that? How hard is it to tamper with them?"

"Can you up the voltage? Yeah, up to a point. It's no high-tech project. Anyone who's had high school physics or knows a little about electronics could do it. And the expensive, new collars are supposedly a hundred percent waterproof. Hunters want something they can leave on a retriever when he hits the water. So waterproof and water-safe are big selling points. The old ones weren't, and if the seal's broken . . . and in this situation, you've got water. Maybe she was standing in it."

"We can look," I said. "On the way out. We can see if there would've been a puddle there, in heavy rain. There was a real downpour, at least in Cambridge, and I gather here, too. Anyway, the burn marks are sort of confusing me because the other thing is that across the street, that woman who's making me the scarf for Buck—Marcia Brawley—has one of those damned electronic fences. Actually, you know what's the worst thing about it? These people, the Brawleys, have a border collie. Jesus, what kind of person would give electric shocks to a border collie? Border collies are about ten times as intelligent and sensitive as most people."

"They vary," he said. "But, in general, they're real bright." He rubbed Lady's head. "It's more apt to be these guys."

"Pointers?"

"Bird dogs. Hounds. Hunting dogs all work at a distance."

"Steve, I saw this dog, and what he does is, when he gets near the edge of the lawn, he acts really strange. He stops and backs up. But also, it's hard to describe, but he has an odd look. Their eyes are always eerie, but he looks abnormal, not like a border collie. Anyway, his collar is definitely not a regular collar. It's light-colored, flat, with a sort of box. Obviously, it's a shock collar. So I assumed it's one of those damned electronic systems, with wire buried around the perimeter of the yard. I know they work on radio waves. That's what triggers the shock. When the dog gets in range of the wire, the collar picks up the radio waves, and the collar gets a signal to give a shock. Right? So what I thought was, maybe the system got screwed up, and the radio signals got to Rose's pacemaker. But that can't be right, because it wouldn't burn. It would make the pacemaker go berserk, but it wouldn't burn her hand."

"So why . . . ?"

Why. Yeah. I just put this together today, at the match. Look, the school where Rose taught, Case, sounds like a real

neighborhood school. And it's small. There's only one kindergarten, and that's what Rose taught. At Jack's, just after she
died, I heard that maybe four years ago, she had a kid in her
class, and she thought he was being abused. Physically. And she
filed this charge or something against the parents, a 51A. Someone there sort of blurted out that the parents were real Newton
types, the last people you'd expect. He said they were Mr. and
Mrs. Newton. Among other things, they were the presidents of
the PTA. And what I put together today is that it was the Brawleys, the same people. Someone was talking about how Marcia
Brawley did all this stuff, and one of the things was being president of the PTA, and Marcia Brawley's kid is the right age. So
at first I thought, well, maybe there was a weird accident, right?
Electric storm, radio waves, Rose's pacemaker, and the signal
accidentally gets to her. But if the signal comes from these people, that's just too much of a coincidence. She accuses them of
child abuse, she files this 51A, and it just so happens to be their
electronic fence. And since they lived right across the street
from the tennis courts, and they knew her, they'd know she'd
be there. They'd've seen her training there. So they had this
grudge against her, and they had this damned fence. But it just
doesn't compute, not with the burn marks."

"When was it this happened? Four years ago?"

"Something like that."

"Why would they wait four years?"

"I don't know. But I agree. Either they would've done something then, or you'd think they'd mostly want to forget it. And
what would they get out of it? There are some kinds of hurts
that can smolder for a long time, and if people want revenge,
they don't care when. But this? And while we're on the subject,
I've been thinking about this judge Rose reported to the AKC.
Sam Martori. Rose could be pretty tough. She reported him for
ethical violations. It was in the *Gazette* and everything, and it
wasn't all that long ago. But this thing with the Brawleys isn't
something like that. It just doesn't fit. Anyway, that fence
wouldn't leave burn marks, not on her. Even if the radio waves
somehow got *sent* in her direction, they might screw up the
pacemaker, but they wouldn't burn her hand."

"Are you sure it's that kind of system?"

"What other kind is there?"

"A plain old shock collar. With a transmitter."

"Right. That's possible. You hire a guy to come to the house and train the dog not to cross the boundary. Or you do it yourself. But I don't think it works all that well, at least not the way those fences do. I'll tell you, whatever's been done to this dog is something that works. But it is possible."

"Holly, how sure are you that these are even the same people?"

"Pretty sure. How many PTA presidents are there? And don't forget, these are people who've done something god-awful to a border collie. A border collie! That part all fits. But am I totally sure? No. Even if they have a regular shock collar, what's bothering me is that . . . It isn't so much that they didn't have anything to gain. It's that a lot of other people did."

"Like?"

"Heather Ross. You know who she is? You've seen her at shows, in Open and Utility. Silver-haired woman with a silver standard poodle, fabulous obedience dog."

He nodded. "A robot."

Maybe you know that that's a backhanded compliment. A robot is a dog that works precisely but mechanically, without dash and spirit.

"Not really," I said. "And he's kind of a monster out of the ring. Anyway, she and Rose go way back, probably thirty or forty years, for all I know, a long time. And I think they were major rivals all along. You know what those poodle people are like."

"Unlike the golden retriever people." His voice smiled.

I defended myself. "You think you're kidding, but you're not. They're much more competitive. And Heather and Abbey—that's her daughter—did know about the pacemaker. I know that for sure. And in the ring, Rose was a threat, she really was. And for all I know, there was other stuff, too, old stuff. I've thought a whole lot about it. Competition *is* one thing I understand."

We were climbing up a steep, rough trail. Lady, Steve's pointer bitch, was following a yard or two behind us, India had temporarily vanished, and Rowdy and Kimi were ahead of us. Rowdy'd reached the top of the hill and was surveying it as his domain while Kimi made wild dashes through piles of leaves and brush.

"I know, I know," I added, pointing to my dogs. "They aren't exactly Gaines Top Dog material, but . . ."

Most of the time, Steve is a serious guy. He approaches people, dogs, cats, and all other creatures with an attitude of grave interest. His smile is never automatic—it always means something—and when he laughs, as he did then, his eyes crinkle and radiate glee.

"Well, okay," I conceded, "but I didn't always have malamutes, and I do know how it feels. And I have mixed feelings about it. But Heather doesn't. A couple of days after Rose died, she was proposing a memorial trophy designed for her to win herself, and she was totally unabashed about it. And they double handle, Heather and Abbey. She probably tapes liver to her thigh, for all I know." That's the left thigh, at dog-nose level, right where his head goes when he's heeling perfectly. Food is, of course, prohibited in the ring, but the stewards don't do a strip search. "People are always saying that she'd do anything."

"That doesn't mean a thing," he said. "People are always saying that about top handlers."

"I know! But maybe it's no joke. And she does have a shock collar. Abbey told me so. I'm sure she hardly ever uses it, and when she does, she knows exactly what she's doing, but she has one. And she'd have known Rose would be there. Rose always talked about training at the tennis courts. Not just there, of course, but it was her regular place. It was no secret. That's how Nonantum happened to get the park, because Rose always trained there, so she knew about it. Heather and Abbey must've known. But I don't know if the competition was actually cutthroat, and I have no idea whether she was really there. Or whether both of them were, Heather and Abbey, because if they had something to do with this, that's how I see it: double handling, the old mother and daughter act."

"They go way back? Did Rose leave anything to Heather? Was there money?"

I shook my head. "Not that I've heard, though she did have money of her own. She started some kind of scholarship, but apparently, the rest went to Jack. That's another thing. You want to know who benefited? Not that Jack did, exactly, but if you go there now, it's a kind of family reunion. You remember, I told you, when he married Rose, his family sat shiva for him? Now all of a sudden, he's back in the family. Or they're back with him. And maybe this is totally off base, but his sister, Charlotte Zager? She's a dentist, right? In Newton. And her son, what's his name, Don, is a vet. Also in Newton. You know him?"

"Only that he's, uh, he's a holistic veterinarian. He does acupuncture. Homeopathy. It's real trendy now, acupuncture, all that. Most of it's harmless. Maybe it helps."

"If it's so trendy, you'd think his clinic would show it, and it doesn't. It makes yours look like Mass. General, at least from the outside. And that's the point. No, actually, that's the question. What we have is, Charlotte Zager's a dentist, okay? Now, who knows more about electricity and water? That's what dentists do all day. They use electrical equipment in wet places. And her son? He happens to be a veterinarian. So maybe people who use shock collars don't come to you, but he'd know these things exist, and he'd know where to buy one. If he subscribes to *Dog's Life* for the waiting room, he's on a million mailing lists, and he gets armloads of catalogs, and most of them sell these damned things. At a minimum, he'd see the ads. And the point is, with Rose dead, Jack inherits her money, not that he needed it, I think, but his sister and his nephew inherit a rich relative. If Don needs money to fix up his clinic—and it looks as if he does—Jack is probably going to come through. He's kind. He's generous. He's exactly the kind of person you could count on to give you what he had. The nephew wouldn't necessarily know that, but his own sister would. And she'd've known he wouldn't refuse to see them or anything, too. I mean, he didn't. There they are."

"The family kicked him out? There was no contact?"

"None, I think."

"Then tell me something. How are they supposed to have known who Rose was? How would they recognize her?"

"They all live here, in Newton. Sometime or other, they must've seen each other, on the street, in a store. Charlotte would recognize Jack, obviously, and if she kept seeing the same woman with him? But there is one sort of related hitch, which is about the tennis courts. I just don't see how they would've known Rose went there, that she always trained there. But it's possible. Speaking of which, we're almost back there, I think. I'm pretty sure the field's over this hill. I'd better get the dogs. Okay, so when we get to the tennis courts, we take a look at

the door. And if the border collie, Rascal, is out, across the
street, I want you to take a look at him and tell me what you
think. And there's also . . . Well, there's more."

"With you, there always is," he said.

Chapter 19

"THAT'S the original," I told Steve. Pale pink-red showed through the scrubbed, whitened blotch on the wall as if someone had scoured Bon Ami into dried blood. "Mine's a mere reproduction."

"The house backs onto the woods?" He tilted his head toward the maze of trails and trees.

"Faces them. It's across the street. But there isn't a house across from it, just the woods and sort of a low fieldstone wall, not like this. The whole block across from the Englemans' is woods, no houses."

"But it'd be easy enough . . ."

"Cross the street and jump over the wall. Step over it. And there'd hardly be any objection from home, if they even knew about it. Well, from the mother, anyway." I narrowed my eyes, hunched my shoulders, and mimicked Edna's smug, bigoted whine: "What kind of a name *is* 'Winter,' anyway?"

"That doesn't have to mean Jewish or not," said Steve, rubbing a hand up and down Lady's shoulder. Of our four dogs, she was the only clingy one, an insatiably love-hungry but endlessly lovable pointer.

"No. It just usually does because it's usually anti-Semites who want to know. So the question's neutral, but the people aren't. You haven't met Edna Johnson."

"Maybe. Yeah. It's true I never get asked what kind of name 'Delaney' is."

"Of course not, but 'Winter' really can be Jewish. Or lots of things, I guess. I don't know. I don't care. But I do get asked, and, yeah, once in a while, it's probably just curiosity, like

'What kind of dog is that?' But you know what? That doesn't sound neutral if you've got any kind of bull terrier."

"Yeah. Then it's not curiosity. Most of the time."

"Right, because some people are dying to see a real, live pit bull attack someone, and they're disappointed when the dog just stands there acting like any other dog. Some of the time, though, people just want to know what kind of dog it is. Period. But how do you tell?"

Kimi suddenly raced out of the woods, down a hill, and across the field. Her target was one she'd hit before: my left knee. I made for the wall and flattened myself against it. At the last second, she veered, fled back to the center of the field, and flew around and around in narrowing, frenetic circles.

"Jesus," I said. "But you see? In places where people are keeping lots of wolves and hybrids, I'd have to worry. What if the wrong person strolls into the park and sees her like that?"

We decided to take a look at the gate before it got too dark.

The high chain link fence enclosed six courts, one row of three in the area we entered through the gate, then beyond it, another three in a second area separated from the first by yet more chain link. Steve bent down and peered at the gate and the handle, and I took my first inside look at the courts.

"Hey, Steve, watch it," I said. "Keep the dogs out. There are nails all over the place. We better put the dogs in the van. If they get in here, their feet'll be filled with punctures."

Once we'd crated the dogs, we returned to the courts. They were red clay, but I can't imagine that anyone could have played tennis on that powdery, sandy surface. Maybe what's luxurious about clay courts is that they need maintenance. These hadn't had any. The nets were missing, and nails stuck out of long, thin strips of once-white plastic that had originally marked out the lines in the courts. Many of the plastic strips had come loose, and the nails that had tacked them in place now protruded upward.

"How could Rose've trained here?" I said. "Look at it! She'd never have trained here. I don't understand this, because I know she did."

"What's it like back *there*? Maybe it's better. There's a door there, a gate, on the right."

As Steve guessed, the distant row of courts was in much better shape than the first. Like the first, it had no nets and a pretty rough surface, but the white plastic strips were in place, the nails sharp-end-down in the clay.

"Okay," I said. "This is it. Obviously, this is where she trained. She kept Caprice on leash, or at least at heel, and they'd walk through that mess back there. Then once they got in here, she'd shut this second gate. And then it was fine."

"So which gate? Which was the one they found her by?"

"The other one. The one that leads out of the courts. Somebody pointed it out to me, at class. I guess we were all feeling superstitious or something. Nobody really wanted to go near it. Actually, this explains something."

He got it, too. "She's training in here. Between her and that first gate, there's this fence." He rapped his knuckles on the chain link that separated the rows of courts. "And then there's the whole length of the other courts."

"And her mind's on Caprice, right? What's she going to notice?"

If you've never trained a dog for show, maybe you don't understand, but success in the ring is about ninety-nine percent a matter of attention, the dog's and yours, and you lose yourself in your dog. His front feet are misaligned by one inch? Oh-oh. If the judge notices, that's a half point lost. That's where your attention goes, to the off front foot. Two baseball teams show up and start a game? Does it register? Yes. Great natural opportunity to proof the exercise, you think. Two teams of Martians land and launch a game of intergalactic planetball? Another great distraction, nothing more. A strange dog leaps into your training area? Now, that's a real interruption, a break in the fusion. But a little thunder? The threat of rain? Some guy hanging around doing something off there somewhere? Who notices? Not a trainer like Rose Engleman.

"Someone could've wired a bomb to that gate," I said. "Jesus. Basically, someone did."

"Okay," Steve said, "let's walk through it. She finishes up in here. She snaps a lead on the dog, or she calls her to heel. They go through here." He opened the gate to the first set of courts, and we passed through. "Okay, next?"

"Next, they make a sharp right, here, and they go parallel to this center fence, and then down this way toward the gate, because it's a sort of nail-free path." I walked briskly down it because that's how dog trainers are supposed to walk. The AKC says so. "And they get here, and guess what? They're in a puddle."

As I've mentioned, the surface of the court was torn up and rough. In front of the gate was a wide, shallow depression, a dry puddle.

"They're in a puddle," he repeated. "Can't avoid it. And there aren't any nails here. Rule that one out. There aren't any nails for, say, the first two, three yards. Hey, were the dog's feet cut? Punctured?"

"No. I don't think so. No. It was Friday night, and I saw her Sunday. She wasn't limping."

"So she didn't run around in here. Okay, the gate. You see anything?"

I bent down as he'd done before. A flat strip of metal, maybe eight inches long, an inch wide, and quarter of an inch thick, formed the handle. I held it, moved it up and down, and ran the tips of my fingers over it. "Not a thing," I said. "It's smooth."

"It's getting dark now," he said. "Heavy clouds. Rain. You want to go home. You're standing in a puddle. And?"

"And my dog's in the puddle. I'm feeling a little guilty, keeping her out in the rain. I'm thinking about home. And next time, what we're going to work on, how we're going to do it. I'm not thinking about this fence. The gate. The handle."

"So?"

"So I've been here God knows how many times. I don't need to look and see where the handle is. Maybe it's dark enough so I can't see it all that well, anyway. So what? I know where it is. I reach out and grab it."

"And? What do you do if what you grab isn't what you expect? Instead of the handle, there's . . . something else."

"Ah, okay. You know what I'd think? I'd think, Oh, someone found something, something someone lost, and put it here. At this time of year, it wouldn't be a hat or a glove or anything, but it could be—I don't know—a baseball mitt? Anyway, that's what you do if you find something in a park: You put it in a prominent place. You hang it somewhere. So if I reach out and grab the handle, but what I feel is something else—you know what? I'm not scared. I'm not suspicious. If I think anything, I just wonder, Huh, what's this?"

"And if it feels like leather? If you're Rose Engleman, and

you wonder if it's something you dropped, and it feels like leather? A leash."

"Yeah. A leash. Or even a collar. But was she going to stop and think, I better not touch this? Probably it's a shock collar? Of course not. That's the last thing she'd think."

"Hey, Holly, cut it out."

"What?"

"The last thing. You know, that's frivolous. It's not funny."

"Jesus. I didn't mean . . . Steve, I didn't mean it like that."

Chapter 20

"Look, Leah, we had an agreement, right? You train her, you groom her. And you also said you'd give me a hand with the vacuuming, and, in fact, you said you'd do it while I was out. I can see that you've been working on this SAT stuff, and maybe that's important, especially to your parents, but I can't live like this."

"I'll do it! I said I'd do it. See? I'm doing it now." She headed for the broom closet. "Someone called you!" she added as if the news were unprecedented. "Someone named Ample."

"Ample? A man or a woman?"

"Woman."

"Oh." I spelled it out. "A-M-P-L, not Ample. Alaskan Malamute Protection League. Malamute rescue. Did she leave a message?"

"She'll call back."

And after I managed to take a shower without slashing my feet on the razor Leah had left blade-up on the floor of the tub, she did.

"Holly?"

"Yeah?"

"Tina. AMPL? I've got the sweetest little bitch here, and I could use some help."

"Tina, I can't. My male might not be too bad, but not my bitch. Not a chance. But I'd like to help."

"Good. Find me a home for her. You want to hear about her?" She didn't pause. "Four years old, spayed, a little obedience."

When someone says that about a rescue dog, it usually means

the dog sits once in a while whether you tell him or not. See? He understands *sit*.

"Where's she from?"

"Found wandering, picked up by the pound here. They called me."

"What's she look like?"

"Pretty. Nice face, full mask." That's what Kimi has, a full mask, black cap, black goggles around her eyes, a black bar down her nose. Just as Tina suspects, the more these rescue dogs sound like my own, the harder I try to locate homes for them. "Small, maybe sixty pounds, but thin. She's putting on weight, though, and she's such a sweetheart."

Tina had tried and failed to trace the owner and the breeder. The bitch didn't act as if she'd been abused, but maybe she had. Or maybe she'd been neglected, or maybe she'd simply been too big and rambunctious for the people who'd bought a furry little bearlike puppy on the assumption that she'd stay the same size.

"Tina, I'm sorry. I can't think of anyone offhand. But I can ask around." I was thinking about Groucho, Rita's dachshund, about the white on his muzzle and the far-off look in his eyes. How much longer did he have? And how long would Rita insist on waiting? You can hardly blame a therapist for being too psychological, but I was sure she'd insist on devoting a year to working through the loss of Groucho. In the meantime, thousands of wonderful dogs would be destroyed because mourning people weren't yet ready for new dogs. Ask yourself: Would your old dog really mind enough to let my lovely malamutes perish in those gas chambers? Die in agony in research labs? To hell with this sentimental grieving. Your dog just died? Call the American Kennel Club and ask for a referral to Malamute Protection. Save my dogs. Do it now.

Then a face came to mind. "Actually, there is one possibility, a guy I talked to a while ago. I'll give him a call."

When I phoned Jack Engleman's to get Jim O'Brian's phone number, a woman answered.

"Jack is busy at the moment," she said. "This is his sister, Dr. Zager. May I help you?"

"This is Holly Winter," I said. "Fluoride trays? Malamutes? We talked about brushing their teeth?"

"Uh, yes. Is there a problem? With—?"

"No, not at all. Actually, all I need is the number for a guy named Jim O'Brian. He was a student teacher of Rose's. I met him there at Jack's. If there's an address book with phone numbers there, or a Rolodex or something, maybe you could check it for me. I'm trying to place a rescue dog. I thought he might be interested."

Charlotte Zager asked the right question. It boosted my confidence in her: "What kind of a dog is it?"

"A malamute. Spayed female, four years old. Are you—?"

"I might be."

"Do you have any cats?" I always ask that. If the answer's yes, mine is no. Some malamutes like cats. Some like cats for dinner.

"Two," she said. "And Daisy, of course. She's a springer spaniel."

"Then you don't want this dog." I felt like St. Michael weighing her soul and finding that the scales tipped in the wrong direction. Heaven's all right, but it's not quite appropriate for your situation. "I don't know her history, but malamutes aren't usually great with cats." Or other dogs. It's true, but I feel guilty if I say it aloud.

"Oh, well. O'Brian? Here it is. Jim O'Brian." She gave me a number that started with 332, a Newton number. Then we talked a little. My teeth and my dogs were fine, I said. She said that Jack was, too.

By the time I hung up, Leah was in her room reading *Northanger Abbey* aloud to Kimi. I was alone with Rowdy. Alone.

"Alone," I said to him. I sank to the floor, downed him, and massaged his big fur-dripping neck. "We are alone! Savor it, buddy. So the story is, now I have his number and an excuse. Well, okay, not an excuse. He really might like her. So I've got an excuse to call, right? Hey, Jim, how'd you like to adopt a nice malamute bitch, spayed, four years old, no history of abuse, and speaking of which, when you were student-teaching with Rose and she filed that 51A, was it the Brawleys or someone else? Natural, right?"

Jim O'Brian was home when I phoned, and although I led up to the topic of abuse somewhat more indirectly and discreetly than I'd rehearsed with Rowdy, what I had to say was pretty much the same thing. I reminded him that he'd said he might be interested in a rescue dog. Then I described the dog and made sure he didn't have any cats. Finally, I took a deep breath and tried to sound casual. "The woman who's got her doesn't see any sign of abuse. There's no guarantee, and sometimes you can't tell. Maybe it's like that with children, too. Maybe you can't always tell."

"Not always," he agreed.

"Like those people Rose filed the 51A on? Well, something sort of like that can happen with dogs. You'd never suspect the owners, and then suddenly some situation crops up." Remember, I was trying to sound casual and natural, and in the dog world, that means talking on and on about dogs. "And the dog's shaking all over. And you have to wonder what happened the last time he was in that situation, you know? In the back of a van, on a boat, whatever. But I guess with children, you're more apt to see the physical signs, like bruises, like with Zeke Brawley."

"Yeah, judging by the parents, you wouldn't've thought, but even when you see the child, you can't always tell."

If I'd used the wrong name, he'd have corrected me. Whew. He'd certainly remember that he'd been indiscreet, but would he be absolutely sure he'd stopped short of using their names? Did it matter? Rose could've told me.

"Well, with this malamute," I said, "there's no sign, but you never know for sure. Anyway, I hear she's a sweetheart. You want to take a look at her?"

He did. I gave him Tina's number. Was that ethical? Is it right to place an Alaskan malamute, a member of dogdom's royalty, a noble creature of shining intelligence, with a mere human blabbermouth? Sure. Jim O'Brian had loose lips, but the dog wouldn't care.

I hung up and gently rubbed the left side of my head, which felt hot and almost swollen. To own a malamute, you need muscular arms and a strong will. Insensitive ears help, too—outer, not inner. Malamutes woo-woo, but it's nothing compared with the way human beings blah-blah about them on the telephone.

As I was poking in the freezer for an ice pack or, failing that, something to eat, Kimi bounced into the kitchen followed by Leah, who was dressed for bed—or so I assumed—in my red Malamute Power T-shirt, yellow neon running shorts, and a loose white belted top designed for karate practice.

"We have to talk," she announced.

My left ear throbbed, but Rita had recently given me a lecture

on the importance of open communication with adolescents.
"Sure. Of course," I chirped. My voice shifts smoothly into
happy gear. What lubricates my vocal transmission is an Open
obedience exercise called the Drop on Recall. You call the dog,
tell him "Down," and he drops on the spot. Simple? It's inexpli-
cably difficult for dogs, but worse for handlers, because you absolutely must keep that "Down!" light and sunny for all those
hundreds of times it takes the dog to catch on. Sweet and soft
is how you want your voice; cheerful, without a hint of exasper-
ation or impatience. The secret is honesty: Feel happy that the
dog's trying and that the sixteen-year-old is still speaking to
anyone over the age of seventeen. "About?"

Please, not safe sex again. Rita made me raise the topic with
Leah. "What do you know about safe sex?" I'd asked. I'm not
sure whether Leah's answer was comforting or terrifying: "Everything," said Leah.

But this time Leah held a sheaf of little multicolored booklets
in her hand, premium lists and entry blanks for dog shows.
"These," she said. "Are you trying to put this off or something?
We don't have forever. Is there, uh . . ."

"Not at all," I interrupted, shutting the freezer door.

"You think we're not ready?"

"No, of course not. You're ready. You're both ready. And
Kimi's a lot more ready than Rowdy was for his first trial."
With Leah handling her, Kimi was ready. If I'd been handling
her?

"Look, is there some problem here? Is it because she's your
dog? You'd rather—?"

"No," insisted my better self. "Not at all. Let's plan it out."
I went on: "What we're after is who's judging Novice B. Okay?
Any AKC trial is going to have Novice B. So we'll just look
through for the Novice B judge, and then we'll decide, because
judges aren't all the same. In theory, they are, but they aren't."

Leah thumbed through a pale green premium list while I
checked one for an upcoming trial in Vermont.

"This is Mr. Fish," she said.

"Good! He's okay. He isn't too friendly. He won't go out of
his way to make you feel relaxed. But he's very fair. He's a good
judge. He'd be fine. Let's see. There's more than one Mr. Fish,
but I think the other one retired. Let me check."

She handed me the premium list folded open to the page that

showed the obedience classes. I flipped the page to find the judges' full names and addresses. "It's the right Mr. Fish," I assured her. Also on the list was Samuel Martori. "What show is this?"

"Guilford," Leah said.

"Damn, I think that's already . . . Some of these are old. I should've thrown them out. Yeah, this one's already been held. Look, sort through them, will you? Get rid of the ones we've missed. Fish might be judging somewhere else, and there are plenty of other good judges."

Then the date of the Guilford show and trial hit me. It was one of a cluster of three shows, Friday, Saturday, and Sunday. Guilford had been the first, the Friday show. All the shows in the cluster had taken place at the same 4-H grounds in western New York State. Martori had been judging Utility B. And I remembered Heather Ross's brag at class one night: Panache had been high in trial at Guilford.

How far was it from Boston? Vinnie and I had been there more than once, but that had been years ago. Five hours? Maybe more. And one piece of information that's maddeningly absent from the premium lists is the time the judging begins for each class. They do announce dates, of course. On the Friday that Rose Engleman died, Sam Martori had been judging at Guilford, and Heather had been there, too, handling Panache. What time had Utility B been judged? Had Heather and Abbey had enough time to drive back to Newton? And had they driven all that way for one trial? Heather would've entered Saturday, too, I was willing to bet, and probably Sunday. Yet she'd been at Jack's house on Sunday. Why?

But if she'd finished late on Friday afternoon? If Martori had been judging then? And especially if they'd all been in western New York State late on Friday and early on Saturday morning? Well, then Heather, Abbey, and Martori had the same solid alibi.

And they did. Late on Sunday night, I reached Sandi Matson, one of my *Dog's Life* buddies. At Guilford, on Friday, she said, Utility B started in the afternoon. Martori and Heather were both at the Saturday show, too. So why didn't Heather brag about her Saturday score as well as about Guilford? Well, that's obvious: It was a lousy score. Anyway, Saturday didn't even matter, because Sandi has poodles, and poodle people hang out together. She had dinner with Heather and Abbey on Friday night. Martori sat two tables away. While Rose was in Newton training for the last time, they were all in New York State.

Chapter 21

WILLIE Johnson called Leah the next morning on the pretext of asking about an upcoming fun match. Spurred by Rita's strong views on open communication, I used his call as the opportunity to have a frank discussion with Leah about my take on his family. Open is just that, open, according to Rita, two-way and honest, and I was. People who grow up in dysfunctional families have a hard time learning how to act in the rest of the world, I said. Furthermore, this family had a history of violence, and it made me nervous. Leah had probably been talking to Rita, too, because she pointed out that my nervousness was my problem. My hackles went up a little, and I told her about the abuse of one of the dogs and about the fights at the family business, more than I probably had a right to spill. Maybe I was unfair to Willie.

An hour later, while Leah was taking a shower, the front doorbell rang. Hell, roses again, I thought. I prepared a speech for the florist's delivery person: Leah Whitcomb had moved, she wasn't coming back, and I wouldn't accept the flowers.

But when I opened the door, the brown UPS van was pulling away, and a box with a return address in Freeport, Maine, sat on the porch. Good clothes and large, shedding dogs are incompatible, of course, but nevertheless I'd splurged on a summer-weight short-sleeved cotton sweater from L. L. Bean, in a very impractical shade of navy blue, together with a pair of hiking boots. I didn't even open the box before I stashed it in my bedroom closet, out of Leah's view, and shut the door.

A moment later, a heavily betoweled Leah emerged from the bathroom with that incredible glowing hair plaited, wrapped, and wound into an elaborate coiffure suitable for a lady about to be presented to the Court of St. James. Kimi and Rowdy, my own royalty, were daffy about her, anyway, but she'd evidently rubbed some kind of after-bath lotion on her legs and feet, and they ran for her and began licking her skin and wagging their tails.

"Oh, God, no!" she ordered them. "Get away! Holly, get these dogs away! They're getting their fur all over me!"

"Easy, there," I said. "They don't know they're shedding. Come on, guys. I'll be nice to you."

But when she'd layered herself, she was all smiles and pats again. She made up with the dogs and took Kimi out to do some work. In their absence, I called Steve and reached him between patients.

"Look, I've thought of an excuse for you to find out about Don Zager," I said. "The nephew? What you need to do is call him."

"Clever," he replied. "Devious. I'd been thinking of something simple and straightforward. Like calling him."

"Well, so what's your excuse? You don't have one. Were you just going to call up and introduce yourself and say hello? What you need to do is ask about this stuff he does. Tell him you heard he did this alternative veterinary whatever it is, homeopathy, and say you're interested. Why don't you say you might want to refer someone to him?"

He answered patiently and slowly. "I called him this morning," he said one word at a time. He's used to explaining complex veterinary matters to uncomprehending owners. "I called him this morning," he repeated. "He was not available. I left a message. About my interest in acupuncture. He will return the call."

"A step ahead, huh? So when he calls, you also need to raise the subject of shock collars."

"Acupuncture is painless," he said, "or it's supposed to be. I haven't tried it myself, but people swear the needles don't hurt. So I pretend I don't know that, and I say, 'Well, Don, now that we're on the subject of needles, you ever try electric shock?'"

"There is that," I said. "Or what if you ask something about behavior? Like, tell him you have a client with two malamutes that fight, and ask if acupuncture helps. Then we'll at least know if he's a big proponent of shock collars, because if he is, he'll say that's the answer."

"And let him think . . . ? Hell, no. Anyway, we don't know much about him, but we do know he does alternatives, right? You know anything about homeopathy? You know what they use? Powders. Herbs. They call them gentle remedies."

"Okay. A shock collar's not exactly a gentle remedy. Well, we already know he'd know where to get one. So his mother would, too, presumably, if she saw the catalogs. And we know he uses needles. Obviously, he can't be exactly squeamish. I guess mostly what we need is some kind of feel for what he's like, and also some idea of the finances."

"Piece of cake," Steve said. " 'Tell me about acupuncture, and while you're at it, mail me your last year's 1040.' "

"Stop it! What you need to do is commiserate with him. Say something about Cambridge rents, insurance. Think of something to bitch about, and then maybe he'll tell you about how he's trying to pay off his student loans or how he wishes he had some new ultrasound equipment or something. Obviously, you can't drag it out of him, but give him a chance."

I hung up with little hope. Steve either does something or he doesn't. Maybe I should fabricate some ailment in my dogs and ask Zager to cure it. Fine if he prescribed a gentle powder I could throw out, but what if he decided to use needles? Forget it. Steve keeps my dogs up on their shots. Except for that, no one punctures my dogs, acu or otherwise.

In the early evening, Jeff and Lance, the border collie, stopped in. Rowdy and Kimi leapt around. He woo-wooed, but she turned food-protective when Lance's eerie eyes wandered toward her water dish, and I hustled them outside to the fenced-in yard.

Although Leah and I had assembled a tentative list of trials to enter, we hadn't made any definite decision or completed the entry blanks yet. Jeff joined us in reviewing the possibilities, and he and Leah made the final selections. Then I showed both of them how to complete the forms, did Rowdy's myself, and wrote out our checks. Meanwhile, Lance maintained a perfect down-stay, his intelligent head resting on his forepaws, those mesmerizing eyes vigilantly monitoring us and whatever we did. Someday, if I'm ever mature enough to handle that all-seeing gaze, I have to have a border collie. I wondered for a moment about the difficulties of kidnapping one who's been trained not to cross an invisible, torturous boundary. It seemed to me I could surmount them. It also seemed to me that I could be caught and arrested, and that the court would find against me.

"Holly?" Leah startled me. "Are you with us? Are you here?"

My mother's voice and face, with Leah's own tone and cast, brought me back to earth. "Daydreaming," I said. "Are we all set?"

"We are all hungry," Jeff said cutely. "We are all hungry for pizza, and we are all going to bring it in for you, and we are all getting a movie if Rita will let us use her VCR."

As I may have mentioned, I liked the kid a lot.

Chapter 22

"HER jumps," Steve said over Tuesday morning breakfast at my kitchen table.

Most people look their best when they've had eight hours of sleep, but exhaustion becomes him. As soon as he has another veterinarian in the practice with him, his eyes will probably lose that green hue and turn ordinary blue. Their clear, sad expression will get murky and flat. He'll have time to shave. He went on: "What happened to Rose Engleman's jumps and hurdles? They'd have nails."

In case you've never trained beyond Novice, I should mention that for Open, you need a high jump and a set of broad-jump hurdles, and for Utility, both the high jump and a bar jump. Until a few years ago, all jumps were made of wood, and the regulation ones used in trials still are.

"They were those PVC practice jumps," I said. "Plastic. You want another English muffin?"

"Just coffee," he said. "Thanks."

I filled his cup. I don't always pop up and down to wait on him, but he'd been up since three A.M. removing the chewed pieces and metal squeaker of a cheap rubber toy from the intestines of a collie.

"So they were plastic," I said. "I know that's what Rose used, because someone was asking about whether the PVC ones were any good. Someone said Rose used them, and she liked them."

"And they're what? PVC pipe?"

"For the high jump and the bar jump. And the broad-jump hurdles are—I guess it's PVC. Some kind of plastic. I've seen them. In fact, I need to get some. They're totally plastic, except for the canvas used instead of boards on the high jump. They

147

weigh practically nothing. You just throw them in the car or under your arm and go practice wherever you want. There's not a nail in them, nothing metal at all. PVC wouldn't do anything, would it? Even if lightning had struck."

"So we're back to—"

"Yeah, we're back to," I said. "And I suppose the easiest way to get a good look at one is to buy it."

He looked unhappy, but I went to my study, rummaged around, and found some catalogs. The cover of one showed an array of my favorite breeds: a malamute, a border collie, two pointers, and a golden.

"This is the one I hate most," I said. I opened it to the order form. "There's a thirty-day trial period," I said, looking up. "One of us could rush-order one or go to a dealer and buy it, and then we could take a look at it and return it."

"Which one of us did you have in mind?" Steve asked placidly.

"Does it matter?" I said. "Whichever one of us has the money, I guess." Depending on the breed, you can buy one or two purebred dogs for the price of a fancy high-tech shock collar. "You don't have an extra person to feed for the summer, so you're probably less broke than I am."

"You know, Holly, the truth is, I just don't feel comfortable about it." His wonderful, tired eyes looked straight at me. "If you don't mind, I'd rather not do it."

"If you order it, you don't have to put D.V.M. after your name, if that's it," I assured him. "Or don't use your own name. Or pay cash. And we *are* going to return it. They give you all your money back. It's not as if they'd profit from it. We won't be supporting the industry."

"But, uh, it indicates interest. It's a statement that it's okay. Doesn't it seem like that?"

"So you'd rather I . . . ?"

He shrugged.

"Well, the truth is, I don't feel like it, either," I said. "But we do need one, if we want to be really sure. I mean, how easy *are* they to tamper with? The other things we can try with a regular collar, I guess, if we have to. We can figure out how to fasten it to the gate. And see if we can rig it so we can retrieve it from far away, or if we have to go back and get it."

"Any chance of borrowing one?"

"I guess. We must know someone who has one. Well, Heather does, although Abbey was the one who told me about using it. I mean, she didn't say outright that they have one, but she all but did, and I could ask one of them. In fact, I can ask around tonight, at Nonantum. So what'd you find out about Don Zager? Did he call you back?"

Serious people smile better than the rest of us. Lines appeared around Steve's sleepy eyes, and the pupils glittered.

"What does that mean?" I asked. "What does he sound like?"

"The question is where," Steve corrected me. "The answer is California."

"Ah, acupuncture. Alternatives. Okay. It's Cambridge enough, though."

"He isn't. Cambridge is not, uh, mellow."

Cambridge is quick and sharp. It is less strident than New York, but there is nothing soft, gentle, or ripe about it.

"Is Newton?" I said.

"No. But the rents are better."

"So you did get to that! Great. And what did he say?"

"He wasn't too articulate. He doesn't exactly rush to the point of things. He proceeds real slow." This from a person who customarily leaves a two-second pause after every word.

"He sounds brain-injured," I said. I grew up in Maine, but I'm acclimating myself to the intellectual climate here, where any sign of relaxation is considered pathological or lazy. If you don't take work with you on vacation, people eye you as if you ought to see a neurologist.

"He's just, uh, calm," Steve said. "He's had good conventional training. I don't know if there's anything in the rest, but he's real sincere. Friendly. He doesn't sound like a bad guy. Just, like I said, California."

"So what about the rent? Did you get anything else?"

"I said Cambridge was a real interesting place, and he said the rents were high."

"Is that all? Everyone says that. Did he sound as if he wanted you to send him patients?"

"Who doesn't? But he also says he's there temporarily."

"On Washington Street? In Newton?"

"No, he's staying in Newton. He knows people. He grew up there. He's moving to some place in Newton Corner. It isn't ready yet."

"So the financial motive *is* there. If it isn't ready yet, it's new. Or it's being fixed up, right? He did sound as though he's moving up, didn't he? He sounded happy about it?"

"Oh, yeah. He said he'll be real happy to show me what he does, but he wanted me to wait until he's moved. Yeah, it's definitely a move up."

An hour or two after Steve left, Marcia Brawley called about the article I'd rashly proposed writing about her. Larry, her husband, had photographed the Akita wall hanging before the people picked it up. She had a print of that picture for me as well as a couple of others that I just *had* to see. Should she mail them to me? I thanked her, but said that I had a dog training class that night at the park across from her house. I'd pick them up.

In the afternoon, Leah, Emma, Miriam, and Monica went into Harvard Square. Leah returned with an embossed leather cowboy belt she'd found in the markdown bin at Ann Taylor, but the other three had big plastic bags of cotton sweaters, shorts, and pants from the summer sales and darker, heavier back-to-school clothes as well. Was the contrast hard for Leah? I watched and listened in, but her lovely, happy face showed no sign of envy, and her voice was as enthusiastic as if the new clothes had been her own. Then they took over the bathroom to do each other's hair to the accompaniment of a station that every five minutes accurately announced itself as the Blast of Boston. Kimi, Rowdy, and I escaped to the Stanton Library for a few hours of silent work on my column.

When we returned, I wanted to inform Leah that a mere ten minutes of the time she'd devoted to personal vanity would have rid poor Kimi of the worst of the undercoat that was rapidly forming ugly, woolly lumps on her shoulders, loins, and rump, but I'd adopted a new strategy: Say nothing, and let Leah see for herself just how rapidly her pretty Kimi would turn into a shaggy mess. In the meantime, Kimi wouldn't suffer. Blowing her coat didn't bother Kimi. And if I worked her over with a shedding blade when I groomed Rowdy, it wouldn't bother Leah, either. (A shedding blade, by the way, is a loop of serrated metal attached to a handle. If that's news to you and you have a dog that sheds, I've just saved you about a million hours of brushing, combing, and vacuuming.) On Sunday morning before the match, Leah had perfunctorily gone over Kimi with a finishing brush that hadn't touched the undercoat. No one had

groomed her since, and she looked like hell. We had dog training that night. I was counting on Heather Ross or some other
soul of tactlessness to remark what a neglected-looking fright
Kimi had become.

By the time we left for dog training, Kimi's coat looked even
worse than it had in the midafternoon. Loose white and pale
gray guard hairs and undercoat clung to every surface of her
body, and the fur she'd already dropped had revealed the lean,
muscled, wolflike contours usually softened by her thick, rich
coat. When she moved, escaping fur surrounded her as if she
were some skinny spirit dog passing through this reality in a
ghostly cloud. The dark wolf gray on her head, back, and tail
had paled, and, worst of all, the shining almost-black on her
face had faded, washing out the full mask—the cap, the Lone
Ranger goggles, the bar down her nose. Even to me, she looked
almost like someone else's malamute, some stranger's pale gray
dog.

But I said nothing to Leah about grooming Kimi. On the
drive to Newton, I made small talk.

"Nice shirt," I said. "I haven't seen that before."

"Thanks. It's Emma's," she said. I didn't point out that
Emma wouldn't be happy to have it returned with an angora
coating. "Hey, is it okay if I go to Emma's after class?"

"I guess," I said. "But how will you get home?"

"With Jeff."

"Sure. Just be home by eleven or so." It isn't easy to set a
firm curfew for the reincarnation of your own mother. "Eleven-
thirty at the latest."

Chapter 23

WE arrived at the park a few minutes late. I hoped Marcia Brawley wasn't in a talkative mood, but as it turned out, I didn't see her at all. I'd told her I'd stop by for the pictures up at seven. When I got to her front door, she'd left, but a note taped to the mailbox said she'd had to run to the store. It directed me to a big manila envelope that rested behind the screen door. I picked it up and started toward the Bronco, but then saw Leah waving at me. In fact, she was lifting her right arm and bringing her hand to her chest. It's a dog-training signal usually reserved for the dog, but I knew what it meant: "Come!" I crossed the street, and, when I got close enough, heard her call, "Holly? They've started already, and I don't have any money."

With both dogs on leash, she was standing by a card table where a bald, skinny guy from Nonantum was seated on a folding chair and checking people in.

"I do," I said. "Thanks for getting the dogs out. I'll take Rowdy." Then I added to the guy at the desk, "I'll pay for her. Leah Whitcomb, for Bess's class, and I'm Holly Winter, for Tony's."

With no warning, Rowdy suddenly hit the ground and crawled a foot or two, and from under the card table, a ferocious snarl broke out.

"Patton, that'll do," the bald guy told a Rottweiler crouched at his feet where I hadn't noticed him.

"Rowdy, be good," I said, hauling him backward. I handed Leah the envelope. "Here, take these. I need both hands. And watch it. Don't bend them. They're photographs. Rowdy, heel."

He did. Patton retreated with all the compliant goodwill of

153

the original George S. I dug into my purse, fished for cash, and paid.

I don't understand anything about dogs. Malamutes are an Arctic breed, and Rowdy was the first creature of any species I'd ever met who loathed hot weather as much as I did. Yet that evening, Rowdy didn't seem to notice the ninety-degree temperature and the thick, moist air that was crushing my chest. He heeled as pertly as if he'd been enjoying the midwinter chill that invigorates us both. I wouldn't have asked him to jump, but his eyes were pleading.

The sight of a beautiful, athletic dog soaring through the air, independently searching out and taking his dumbbell, then flying back over the jump is breathtaking. That night, Rowdy performed perfectly. When I tossed the dumbbell, I could feel his eagerness, but he waited for the command, and when it came, he took two fluid strides, sprang, cleared the top board, and landed gracefully. He made instantly for the dumbbell, grasped it cleanly by the center bar, flew back over the jump, and ended up directly in front of me, where he sat perfectly straight and waited with infinite patience for me to take his dumbbell, which he hadn't tossed or mouthed once. And his performance on the other exercises was almost as good, if less flashy. I forgot the heat. I wasn't in that park in Newton. I wasn't in Massachusetts. I was off in Rowdyland, which is another name for paradise.

At the end of class, plunked back down on some weedy grass with my four-footed memento of the divine, I found a small crowd of Novice handlers and dogs surrounding Bess Stein, who was sitting in the chair by the card table to dispense advice and answer questions. Jeff and Lance, Leah and Kimi, and Willie Johnson and Righteous were part of her throng. Some of Tony's other people were leaving, but I remembered that, having arrived late, I hadn't helped set up. I also wanted to know what Leah had done with Marcia's photographs. With Rowdy on a down—and, as insurance, hitched to a giant tree, one of the few objects a determined malamute can't budge—I helped someone haul the heavy old wooden high jump to a van someone had driven into the park.

Every dog training club, like every other club in the world, has some members who always pitch in and others who apparently believe themselves entitled to be waited on by the diligent. Heather Ross perhaps felt that her presence was a sufficient contribution, but Abbey usually did more than her fair share, especially since she didn't even train a dog. In any case, when I got to the crowd around Bess, Abbey was trying to worm her way to the table so she could fold it and carry it off. I offered to help her. When we'd finally squeezed through the people and dogs, as we were folding the legs of the table, I took the opportunity to ask her about the shock collar, not by that name, of course.

"You remember a while ago, you mentioned something about using a remote trainer? For squirming on sits and downs."

"Works like a charm," she said.

"I was wondering. Do you have one?"

"You want to borrow it?"

"Just as an experiment," I said truthfully.

"Sure, I guess so. I'll bring it next time."

As we were lifting the table, Willie Johnson, whom I hadn't noticed, stepped in and put a hand on it. "I'll do it," he said nicely. "Where does it go?"

"In that maroon van," I told him. "Thanks."

When he got back, I thanked him again and refrained from asking whether the police had questioned him yet and, if so, what he'd said. Leah finally approached Bess to ask some question I didn't hear, and when Bess had answered her and was turning to Willie, I pushed my way toward Leah and said, "What happened to the pictures?"

"You gave them to me," she said.

Then we started leading the dogs out of the park and toward the street. "I know. But what did you do with them?"

"Put them in the Bronco. I have a key, remember?"

Jeff had crated Lance in the back of his family's big white Oldsmobile wagon, and Leah begged to take Kimi with her, too. I gave in. She and Jeff hauled Kimi's crate from my car to Jeff's, and while I waited for them to finish, I said hello to Monica, who'd shown up to get a ride to Emma's with Jeff and Leah.

Monica was wearing a short-sleeved navy-blue summerweight cotton sweater that looked brand-new.

"Pretty sweater," I told her as I stood holding the dogs' leashes and waiting for Leah to get Kimi. "In fact, I ordered one just like it from L. L. Bean."

"Thanks," Monica said. "Actually, it's Leah's."

Oh, was I slow. Was I trusting.

Leah and Jeff finally finished fitting the crate into the station wagon. Then Jeff got into the driver's seat, Monica opened the front passenger door, and Leah came to get Kimi. I handed her the leash.

"Leah," I whispered. "That sweater. The sweater Monica's wearing? That is *my* new sweater, isn't it? The one that just came today? From L. L. Bean?"

"I was going to tell you," Leah said blithely, "but I thought you might say something."

"Like what? 'You're wearing my sweater'? Leah, I want it back," I said childishly. "I haven't even worn it yet. As a matter of fact, this is the first time I've actually even seen it. And you've let someone else borrow it? Without even asking me?"

"I'm sorry. Holly, really, I *am* sorry."

"I want it back," I repeated.

"Well, I can't ask for it now," Leah said reasonably. "What's she supposed to wear? Nothing?"

"No," I conceded. "I guess not. But I don't like this at all. And remember, eleven-thirty. At the latest."

Chapter 24

"So all I thought was, huh, Monica's got a sweater exactly like mine," I told Steve. "It didn't even occur to me that it was a strange coincidence."

Steve had a big smirk on his face. It had been plastered there ever since I'd outlined the story. The heat and humidity had defeated my rattling old air conditioners and driven us outdoors to the back steps. The dogs and I supposedly share the fenced-in yard, which has a park bench, an iron table, and a pair of cheap white resin chairs as well as a collection of canine furnishings. Unfortunately, though, despite my diligent daily cleanups, the Cambridge midsummer steam bath defeats even the ordinarily effective application of Odormute, Odo Kill, and Outright. In short, the yard stinks.

"And then I actually told her I'd ordered the same one from L. L. Bean," I confessed. "I can't believe I was such a naive jerk. I actually complimented her on *my* sweater."

He thought that was pretty funny, too.

"Which was when she said it was Leah's," I added. "And then I finally caught on. It's probably amazing that I managed to do that."

"But you missed the next step," he said.

"And what was that?" I asked, unmollified.

"Ask her whether you could borrow it. She'd probably've said yes." And he laughed some more and patted Rowdy, who was half asleep on the concrete at the bottom of the steps.

"Sure. Why not? And then Leah was so casual. And practical. It was completely maddening. Was I going to tell this girl to take off the sweater and go naked? And it wasn't her fault. It's not as if she'd stolen it."

"If you'd entered into the spirit of it, it would've been no problem," he said. "You could've traded, right there on the spot."

"Right. On the sidewalk. And the worst of it was, I was just seething, and at the same time, I still didn't want to make a scene. I don't believe in humiliating kids in front of their friends, plus I ended up with this ridiculous feeling that I was being sort of stingy and unreasonable, and if I made a scene, I'd just be making a fool of myself. I mean, there they are, open and generous and free, and I'm constricted and selfish."

"It was right not to say anything," he said.

"Well, I did sort of hiss at Leah, and when she gets home, I'm not going to yell at her, but this is really too much. I know you think it's funny, but it's not as if I had a million new sweaters. Damn it, the dogs wouldn't give away my new sweater. And I know you think it's cute, but I'm waiting up for her, and the second she gets in, we are going to have a serious talk about it."

I leaned down, took Rowdy's muzzle between my hands, and gently ran my fingers over his hot, unhappy nose. I didn't say anything, but he knew what I meant: Summer is not forever. Snow will fall. You will be back in harness.

"At the risk of sounding like Rita," Steve said, "uh . . ."

"Uh, what?"

"It, uh . . . Well, you have been, uh, real willing to turn Kimi over to her."

"Yes," I said rather loudly. "I have. I'm glad you noticed. The Alaskan malamute is not a one-person dog, remember?" Actually, the breed standard needs updating; it says *one-man* dog. "What time is it, anyway?"

"Eleven twenty-four."

"So she has exactly six minutes," I said.

"So why'd you change the subject?"

"I didn't. Kimi's with her."

"Relax," Steve said. "So's Jeff."

At quarter of twelve, Steve was mouthing excuses. At midnight, we started in on flat tires. At twelve-fifteen, we finally got to accidents. I hadn't been so angry since the moment that Danny, one of my goldens, had danced out of the woods at Owls Head with a fat porcupine in his mouth. He kept tossing the damned thing up in the air and catching it, driving more and more quills deeper and deeper into his head, muzzle, mouth, and throat. In spite of the pain, he was delighted with himself. I was furious: How could he hurt himself like that when I loved him so much? What if we missed a quill and infection set in? What if one penetrated his brain? What if he died? Damn him for it. Damn Leah.

"Okay, I've had it," I said. "Now I get on the phone."

Leah and I had agreed that, within reason, she could go pretty much where she pleased. But she had to let me know where it was. And, I should add, we had both kept our parts of the bargain. That evening, for instance, she had dutifully left Emma's phone number and address on the message pad by the kitchen phone. If I'd been less worried, I'd have hesitated to wake up Emma's family in the middle of the night, but, in any case, it was Emma who answered. Leah and Jeff had left at ten-fifteen, she said solemnly.

I believed her. "Did they, um, did they say anything about going somewhere else? McDonald's or somewhere? Someone's house?"

Emma didn't know. She had no idea. Next I tried Jeff's number. An answering machine picked up. I left a message. Then I rang the number again a couple of times in the hope that the ringing would awaken or irk the Cohens, but they evidently slept through or ignored it, if they were home at all.

Then I yelled at Steve. "Damn it all! This is my fault. She looks older than she is, and he seemed like such a responsible kid."

"He is a responsible kid," said Steve. "That's what's frightening. He isn't careless. It isn't like either of them to do this for no good reason."

"Oh, shit. I keep imagining . . . Oh, hell. I mean, nightmares happen. Do you remember—when was it?—a car went into the Charles, and someone drowned? Someone was trapped. Steve, they would *call.* If they had a flat tire or the car broke down, they would call."

"Too much beer?"

"Possibly," I said. "I wouldn't swear they don't drink. But you know, I'd swear they wouldn't drink and drive. I had a long, long talk with Leah about that, and I *know* she'd call me. Rita gave me this thing from Students Against Drunk Driving. It was when I first knew Leah was coming, and I was talking it over with Rita, about Leah using the car. And it's sort of corny, but there's this pledge you both sign. Anyway, Leah thought it was corny, and I thought it was corny, and we both signed it. And we joked about it, but we both meant it. Whatever it is, it isn't that. But some drunk could've been driving another car. I feel sick."

"You would've heard. This number's in her purse or something?"

"Yes."

"You would've been called. Let's not get so alarmed just yet."

"Christ! They could've gone anywhere."

"Holly, come on. Calm down."

"She's not your niece!" She wasn't mine, either, but Steve was kind enough not to remind me that she was only a cousin.

"I know," he said. "Look, it's been a long, hot day. It's possible they fell asleep somewhere. Not at Emma's, obviously. At Jeff's? In the car?"

"Why would they . . . ? I mean, they could come here."

"They wouldn't be alone," he said.

"I wouldn't care."

"They don't necessarily know that. Do they?"

"Maybe not. I can't believe I was upset about the stupid sweater. I mean, here she is. She's a wonderful kid. She's cheerful. She has a beautiful disposition. She's friendly, smart, sensitive. She reads Jane Austen. She studies for her SATs. She doesn't do drugs. She's a genius with dogs. And what do I do? I get livid because she's generous, basically. You thought it was funny, but did I lighten up? No, not me. Steve, you don't think I scared her away? That I made her afraid to come home?"

"Not a chance," he said. "There are kids who'd be afraid to come home after something like that, and there are people who'd make them afraid. But she's not like that, and you aren't. Forget it."

"So what do we do? Call the police?"

"To report she's an hour late?"

"There is that."

What we did was a little hard on Rita, who'd gone to sleep hours earlier and had clients scheduled for the next morning, but who wrapped herself in a flowered silk robe and settled on the couch in my hot living room to listen for Leah herself, we hoped, or for the phone. Then Steve and I put Rowdy in the

Bronco and drove to Newton. We followed the river, the route Leah and I always used, but we took it very slowly. The Charles looked oily-dark under the black sky, but nowhere between Cambridge and Newton were there the ambulances I feared. No Oldsmobile station wagon was being hauled out of the water. Officers of the Metropolitan District Commission were not blocking traffic on Storrow Drive to make way for tow trucks and rescue vans. On Soldiers Field Road across from Martignetti's, a cruiser idled peacefully, a speed trap catching nothing. I pulled over, and Steve awoke the dozing trooper. Maybe no news should've felt like good news, but it didn't. It felt like no news.

In Newton Corner, I found a phone booth. Rita had heard nothing. The Cohens' answering machine was still operating efficiently. Their street, Beechcliffe, appeared on the Newton map in my dog-show-tattered guide to the communities of eastern Massachusetts. It was only eight or ten blocks from Eliot Park and the Eliot Woods, but, as it turned out, close only on foot. Park Street was one-way the wrong way, and so were what seemed like the next ten turns we tried to make. We eventually ended up on a street I knew, the one that led past the park entrance. According to the map, that street led to another that led to Beechcliffe.

But we never got that far.

"Slow down," Steve said when we were opposite the park entrance. "Pull over, would you? I want to take a quick look."

"Steve, they aren't going to be there."

"Hey," he said. "Were you ever a sixteen-year-old boy?"

He hopped out, ambled into the field, then trotted back.

"Drive in," he said. "When you get out, leave the headlights on."

They shone on the Oldsmobile wagon. The window next to the driver's seat was shattered. Most of the glass had fallen out. I couldn't see Leah or Jeff or Kimi. I couldn't see anyone but Steve.

Chapter 25

"LEAH? Jeff?" I bellowed, narrowing my eyes and peering into the blackness of the park. "Kimi, come! Honest to God, their driver's licenses aren't even valid after one. I don't know how she thought she was going to get home, and his parents are just going to be thrilled to see what's happened to the car. Leah!"

Steve is more methodical than I am. While I'd been hollering and talking, he'd been tramping in slow, ever-widening circles around the station wagon, his head lowered. Then he stopped suddenly, dropped to the ground just beyond the range of the headlights, and said softly, "Holy shit." He said it again before his emergency mode kicked in. "This is a serious head injury. Get an ambulance. Run to those houses over there. Break a door down if you have to. Get an ambulance."

"Leah?"

"Jeff. Run, will you? Holly, run like hell."

I did. Impulse took me to the doors of the people I knew, first the heavy blond oak of the Donovans' darkened Victorian, where I leaned on the bell, slammed an elaborate wrought-iron lion's head knocker, and shouted, then the simpler aluminum combination screen door of the Brawleys' Dutch Colonial, where the first-floor lights were on. I rang the bell, pounded on the aluminum door frame, and was about to head for the front windows and probably break one when a belligerent-looking, red-faced guy with a head of black curls opened both the door and his mouth.

I didn't wait for him to ask what the hell was going on, but shouted to Marcia Brawley, who appeared behind him with a group of other people who looked as if they'd shared drinks before dinner, wine with it, and brandy ever since. "Marcia, get an ambulance." My breath was coming hard. "Across the street. Right away. Hurry up! And find a doctor fast. Wake someone up."

I turned tail, sprang down the walk and back across the street, and, with the bizarre sense of calm that emergencies induce, got into the Bronco and moved it so the headlights shone on Steve and Jeff, who was stretched out on his back. Even from inside the car, I could see the blood, but that icy practicality stayed with me. A fact came to me: Head wounds bleed. All head wounds bleed a lot, even minor ones. I also remembered that in the far back of the Bronco was a torn and dirty blanket I kept spreading out in a futile effort to protect the interior from dog fur. I got out of the driver's seat, moved to the rear of the car, pushed a curious, nuzzling Rowdy aside and off the grubby, hairy blanket, and shut the tailgate. As I moved toward Steve and Jeff, some pointless urge made me shake the blanket in the air and fold it roughly, as if neatness could improve Jeff's chances of survival. Or maybe it seemed indecent to offer him a filthy shroud.

When I reached them, I handed Steve the blanket, then knelt on the ground by Jeff. His whole head was bloody, those thick, dark-gold curls saturated, his face stained red, one cheek bruised purple. He looked about twelve years old, a gory, beaten angel. "Is he . . . ?"

"Alive," Steve said quietly, spreading the blanket over Jeff.

"They're calling an ambulance, and I've got them looking for any doctors around here. It's Newton. There've got to be ten doctors on the block. Is there anything . . . ?"

"Not a thing," Steve said.

"Then I'm looking for Leah."

"Not on your life," he ordered me.

"I have to. I'll take Rowdy. We'll start with the field. The tennis courts." I hated to hear myself say the words.

"Oh, Christ," he said. "A cruiser'll get here before the ambulance, and then I'll . . ."

I didn't hear the rest. I retrieved a flashlight from the glove compartment of the Bronco, got Rowdy out of the back, snapped on his leash, and started searching and calling. A rapid, easy survey of the tennis courts and the field showed no sign of Leah or Kimi. I cursed myself for never training Rowdy to track. Like every other dog, he could pick up and follow a scent, but I had no way to tell him *which* scent mattered, which to seek, which to follow. For all my obedience-titled partner knew, I'd dropped my car keys or was after someone's lost cat. The flat, open, grassy field was empty, I was sure, but Leah and Kimi, my beautiful cousin and my beautiful dog, could be lying in any of those clumps of shrubby vegetation surrounding it.

Rowdy was no tracker. Even so, as I quickly traced the perimeter of the field, shining the flashlight's beam into the blackness of the weeds, I gave him the full six feet of lead instead of calling him to heel. He didn't understand that I was searching for our own pack, of course, but I trusted him to recognize the slightest sound or scent of his own. His big, wedge-shaped ears were erect but relaxed. Or was he perking them up? Furrowing his forehead? I kept moving the light from the bushes to his head. Were the ears starting to flatten? I'd call loudly for Leah and try to summon Kimi. Then I'd be silent, listening, giving Rowdy the silence he needed to hear the rush of air into lungs, the beat of familiar hearts.

At the far end of the field, where the trail that Rowdy had taken with Steve and me and the other dogs led into the woods, those pretty wedge ears folded, his head dropped about a foot toward the ground, and his lovely white tail swayed over his back with a new beat.

"Good boy," I told him, although it seemed likely that he'd merely picked up our old route. Sled dogs like to retrace familiar paths. "Is this it? Let's give it a try."

I grew up in Maine. If I'd been frightened of woods, I'd have died of heart failure before the age of five. But city woods are different from the Maine woods, which is exactly what makes city people uneasy about real wilderness. City people get nervous when they realize they're alone in the woods. I get nervous if I think I'm not. Trees don't mug anyone. Wild animals—the occasional aberrant bear excepted—avoid people. What I don't like about city woods is that with the exception of a few squirrels and raccoons, the wild animals are human.

And these were city woods. The path we followed was narrow but heavily packed down. As we moved along it, I played the flashlight beam back and forth on either side. Here and there, beer cans reflected it back.

"Leah!" I shouted. "Leah! Can you hear me? Kimi, come! Kimi, good girl! Come!" I whistled and clapped my hands, but the only response I got was the wagging of Rowdy's tail and an extra bounce in his gait.

I stopped and rested a sweaty palm on Rowdy's back to keep him still while I listened for any nearby sound that might stand out against the dull background hum: the deadened whoosh of cars and trucks passing along the Mass. Pike, the vague, indistinguishable almost-nothing of thousands of air conditioners, refrigerators, and packed suburban freezers dutifully fighting the heat. Then a siren broke through the white noise and grew steadily louder; the ambulance or a heralding police cruiser was on its way.

"Let's go, boy," I said quietly. Sweat was dribbling down my neck and back, and when I wiped a hand over my throat, I rubbed in dog fur. I took a couple of long strides ahead, but Rowdy lagged briefly to check something out, a gum wrapper, maybe, or the irresistibly fetid odor of something decaying under a bed of leaves. The flashlight, thanks be in equal parts to God, Eveready, and L. L. Bean, threw a bright, wide spot ahead of me.

"Rowdy!" I smacked my lips. "Let's go!"

I tugged on his leash, and he trailed after me. I flashed the light back to assure myself that whatever had held his attention was something meaningless to me, then shot the beam ahead and ran it back and forth across the path. As if the bright spot were spontaneously halting its own movement, the light froze on a bit of white something that clung to a low branch. I yanked Rowdy ahead and reached for what turned out to be a clump of woolly dog fur, and not from just any dog. I held it to Rowdy's nose and then dug my hand deeply and joyfully into the thick ruff around his powerful neck. Kimi had inadvertently left us a sign, a bit of undercoat on the tip of a branch about a foot and a half above the ground. She had walked or run by here. And if either of my dogs had lost that bit of undercoat on our Sunday walk, it seemed to me, the wind would have blown it from where it rested loosely on the tip of that branch.

But of Leah, there was no sign. On Sunday, Kimi had performed her wild, circling dance of freedom in the open field. She could be doing an encore now, leaping and dashing through the woods, free of human restraint. And Leah could be lying anywhere, a yard or two from the trail. Or far away.

But I thought not. The Brawleys had been home, and from

the looks of their guests, the whole group had been there all evening. No one runs out in the middle of a dinner party to smash a car window, attack the driver, and do God knows what with a sixteen-year-old and a big dog, only to stroll back in and rejoin the guests for brandy. And I had a sense of where we were heading, such a strong, clear sense that I broke into a run.

It's dangerous to take a malamute running in the heat. I slowed to a jog, but Rowdy had caught my spirit and forged ahead, pulling as if he'd been trained for pack ice instead of the show ring.

"Easy there," I called to him. "Slow down." Then I braced myself and made him halt for a few seconds while I ran the light over a triple fork in the path ahead. It seemed to me that the trail we wanted was the one to the right. Or straight ahead?

"Which way, boy?" I asked confidently, but felt as though I might as well have flipped a coin. He hadn't been taught to track. I'd meant to do it someday. I'd been busy. I'd been lazy. Rowdy'd choose a path for us, of course, but he might head us directly toward the backyard hutch of some family's pet rabbits or take us to the nearest bitch in season.

Even so, I let his lead go loose and tried to let him pick the trail on his own. Trouble reaching decisions? Forget those management courses. Get a malamute. Doubt never crosses a mal's mind. Rowdy turned right. Did he smell something? Or had he merely read my mind? I didn't know, but I followed him. Only a minute or two later, when I hauled him in, stopped briefly, and ran the light over the low branches ahead of us, I felt ashamed of having doubted him. Now that I was searching for them, the wisps of Kimi's undercoat on the low branches were impossible to miss. We tore ahead.

Our run ended sooner than I'd expected. Rowdy and I stood in a small clearing. The trail forked. One path climbed sharply uphill to our right, another wandered ahead. But to our left was a low, rough fieldstone wall overgrown with vines and weeds. A streetlamp shone nearby. We were directly across the street from Jack Engleman's house.

Chapter 26

I once had a hundred-pound dog named Rafe who was afraid of thunder. At the first rumble, he'd start shaking and salivating. My presence was his only comfort. Whenever a storm hit during the night, he'd cannonball into my bed and quiver so powerfully that the mattress would vibrate. I'd dream I was sleeping in a cheap motel with a Magic Fingers and an endless supply of quarters. Rafe was also scared of elevators, garbage trucks, letter carriers, veterinarians, sirens, whistles, and bicycles. My anxiety, however slight, instantly communicated itself to my poor Rafe; any trivial worry of mine became Rafe's terror.

Rowdy was no Rafe, but their attitudes toward danger were equally senseless: Rafe feared everything, and Rowdy feared nothing. I don't think he could even grasp the concept of fear. As we paused in that little clearing in the woods across from Jack's house, for instance, he probably misinterpreted the tension in my body, the rapid beating of my heart, and the catches in my breath as signs of the joyous anticipation he always felt himself at the prospect of an imminent slash-and-tear dog fight.

I took a deep breath, blew it out, turned off the flashlight, and clambered over the wall ahead of Rowdy, who cleared it in one bound. Just as he landed, a clap of thunder rolled and a summer torrent let loose as if his agile leap had shaken the earth and ripped open the sky. No lights showed on the first floor of Jack Engleman's house, but a bright glow radiated from the second story on the side facing the driveway and the Johnsons' house.

"Rowdy, this way," I called softly as I took a few wet steps along the edge of the pavement and tugged on his lead. "This way."

The water, I thought. He'd always hated it. The first baths I'd forced on him had been battles of will, and, even now, he'd howl when I scrubbed his underbelly. I'd seen him go swimming only once, when Kimi had accidentally knocked him off the dock and into the pond at Owls Head. He'd immediately rushed out, shaken himself off, and spent the next ten minutes tearing wildly around in indignant protest. But this was nothing, a shallow puddle, and, after all, he wasn't afraid of water. He simply loathed it.

"Rowdy, this way," I repeated insistently, and was about to call him to heel when my conscience pricked me. I remembered the First Commandment of the late St. Milo Pearsall, founder of modern obedience methods: Thou shalt listen to thy Dog and see things from His point of view.

"What is it?" I tried to sound faithful. Even if he'd been tracking the scent through the woods, hadn't the downpour washed it away? Or was it something he could hear? Or simply the familiarity of Jack Engleman's house, the memory that we'd been here before? Like all good sled dogs, he always preferred the known trail to the unknown and balked whenever I wanted us to detour instead of retrace our steps. "Go on," I told him, anyway.

He pranced happily across the street, avoided a puddle under the streetlamp in front of Jack's house, and headed confidently down the driveway. Like the dutiful golden retriever I was born to be, I followed at the end of the leash. That Friday night, I thought. Rose and Caprice went to the tennis courts. No dog trainer himself, Jack stayed home. Home alone? Home at all? Had anyone asked? I hadn't. The question had never even occurred to me.

The blacktop ended at a two-car garage. Its doors were closed, but Rowdy had no interest in them. He circled knowingly to the side of the building, where a large plastic trash barrel had been knocked over, its cover pried off, its contents strewn around. For the second that I trusted Rowdy, I was afraid to look. Then my self-confidence returned and, with it, the chagrined realization that his only practiced tracking skill was a keen nose for—oh, God, yes—food. The flashlight, turned quickly on and off, showed the shredded remains of a white plastic trash bag and numerous bits of crumpled aluminum foil that stank of what smelled like Camembert but may only have been

overripe Brie. Through thunder and rain, my noble lead dog
had guided us swiftly and safely along the track of the last rac-
coon that had raided Jack Engleman's garbage.

Rowdy buried his nose in a large sheet of foil. His paws held
it securely on the ground while his tongue scoured off every last
globule of rancid butterfat.

"Drop it," I said firmly.

He'd been trained to give his dumbbell on command, but obedience dumbbells aren't coated with cheese. He ignored me. I
knew I could pin him, force my fingers in back of his molars,
and wedge his jaw open. I considered hauling him away by
force. The Alaskan malamute is not a giant breed. I outweighed
him by all of thirty pounds, and he was probably a mere ten
or twenty times as strong as I was. He wasn't even wearing a
training collar. Between crashes of thunder, I listened to his
tongue persistently lap the foil. Rain was hitting the trash bar-
rels in loud pops, and water gushed noisily down a spout on
the side of the garage.

Leah and Kimi. Leah and Kimi. And he was feasting on
cheese.

I must have cast my eyes upward in search of heavenly inspi-
ration, but the help I found, if you can call it help, was entirely
mundane. The windows of Jack's house, as I may have mentioned, were designed to look exotically and quaintly baronial.
Except for the leaded-glass trim by the door, the windows in
the front of the house were metal casements with dozens of tiny
clear panes, and at the back of the house, in the remodeled
kitchen where Jack and I had studied the blurred example of
Rose's incompetent photography, large sheets of plate glass al-
ternated with French doors.

The three illuminated windows on the second floor, though,
the ones that faced the Johnsons' yard, were like giant versions
of the small leaded-glass panels in front. Although there were
lights on inside, I couldn't see into the house through the elaborate patterns of yellow, orange, green, and blue that were, I suppose, meant to suggest the stained glass in the private chapel
of some small chateau. One of the windows stood slightly open,
like a door propped ajar, but all I could see through the bright
rectangle was a patch of wallpaper. The windows, then, were
casements, like the ones on the front of the house. They opened.
Rose had stood at one of these to take that blurred photograph.

It might well have been snapped from behind a closed window, but through a pane of clear glass, not through this yellow, orange, green, and blue. The snapshot's colors had been natural, obviously unfiltered. To take the picture, Rose had stood by one of those windows, all right. But the window had been open to give her and her camera an unimpeded view out. Her subject had had an equally good view in. Anyone in greater Boston who read *The Globe* or *The Herald* or who watched the local news or listened to the radio—in other words, almost everyone—knew about the man who went to jail because his smart, effective neighbor did something more than report abuse. That neighbor took pictures of the man beating his dog. In all the reports, that was the point of the story: The man got locked up because the neighbor had solid evidence.

"Rowdy, drop it!" I ordered him, and this time, he heard me. I was born a golden, but lately I'd crossed the breed boundary and become at least half malamute. "Drop it!" I whispered. That's supposed to be the way to get someone to listen, isn't it? With dogs, it's worth a try. So are speed and surprise. I stomped on the piece of foil, lunged for it, and snatched it up and out of his reach. Then I crushed it in my left hand, buried it in my closed fist, and held it flat against my waist, which is a permissible place to put your left hand when you're heeling a dog in the obedience ring. "Rowdy, heel!" I said softly. In training, of course, what's in your fist is liver, cheese, or IAMS dry cat food, but the ball of foil worked fine. Rowdy swung to my left side and, in spite of the wet ground, sat nicely, with his front feet even and his eyes fixed on my face. "Good boy," I said. Thou shalt never, ever forget to praise thy Dog.

I stepped off on my left foot, then switched to an AKC regulation fast pace that took us to the Johnsons' front door in about ten seconds. Except for a low-wattage flood somewhere at the end of their driveway and a pale glow from a cellar window, the house looked completely dark. I rested my entire palm on all of the buttons of the plastic speaker box by the front door and then pounded on the door. Somewhere inside, a dog barked. Rowdy growled a low reply. Then the rain, which had let up a little, began pouring down, and the thunder started up again. My pounding on the door sounded like rattling-metal imitation thunder in a poorly produced radio play, but I wasn't sure that anyone inside could tell it from the real thing. I leaned on the buttons again. The dog's barking was closer this time, much closer. The speaker crackled. I heard nervous, high-pitched breathing. Edna.

"Open up!" I ordered her calmly and firmly. Over the years, I've had a little practice in issuing orders, but I suppose that welcoming visitors was a trick she hadn't mastered yet.

"Let me in," I said as if I expected her to do it.

That didn't work, either. As an obedience prospect, Edna Johnson rated somewhere below poor, but that's probably one of the nicest things anyone's ever said about her. The dog barked again, and I expected Rowdy to roar back and scrape at the door, but something else caught his attention. Hitting the end of his leash, he almost caught me off balance, but I held on and ran after him.

"Easy," I said, nearly falling on the slippery lawn. "Rowdy, wait."

"Leah!" I shouted over the thunder. "Kimi! Leah, yell! Where are you? Leah!" But the dog inside was still barking, and the renewed rain had brought with it a strong wind that rattled loose objects unidentifiable in the dark and blew through the hundreds of Norway maples that line every street in Newton. "Leah! Leah, where are you?"

But I knew she couldn't hear me. Or could she? Was she answering me? It was useless. I heard nothing but the dog and the storm. I tossed the slimy ball of foil into the air, grabbed Rowdy's leash with both hands, and held on.

Then I tripped on something and hit the soggy lawn hard. The fall knocked the wind out of my chest and buried my face in the muddy unmown grass, but I kept my hold on Rowdy's leash and brought him to a halt. The damned rope. I'd forgotten it. Kaiser was kept here sometimes, tied up where he could bark and growl only a few yards from Jack's backyard. I stood up and wiped my hands on my drenched jeans. Rowdy started off again at a slow trot. Following him had now yielded me one bag of garbage and one bad fall.

He pulled me to the back of the Johnsons' house, where the rough, pitted blacktop ended at the closed, windowless doors to a basement garage, but also widened into a small parking lot that held a white delivery van and a mud-colored American sedan. The pale floodlight I'd noticed before was mounted above the doors.

More rotten cheese, I thought; another stop on this ludicrous trash-barrel odyssey. Here, though, were no garbage pails, no torn plastic bags, no scraps of foil, no bits of rotten cheese. The rain had turned to an even mist that hung in the air. Thunder rolled. Suddenly, sheet lightning caught the billions of tiny droplets in the air around Rowdy, who took a couple of quick steps to one of the garage doors and began raking the rough wood with his right forepaw and whining at me. The two-car garage had two sets of old-fashioned double doors, the ones that pull out instead of swinging up overhead. I grabbed a handle on the door that Rowdy was scraping and pulled hard, but it didn't budge. He kept whining at me. I stopped yanking and pressed my ear against the door. Deep, angry male voices rumbled distantly. Leah screamed.

Chapter 27

THE car or the van would have broken down the garage doors, but both vehicles were locked. My frantic search for keys stashed in those little magnetic metal boxes revealed none. Rowdy was impatient, whinnying at me and tugging at his leash. The damned leash was strong, but it was a standard six-foot training lead, way too short. Besides, although he'd pull willingly enough with the leash snapped to his collar, the harder he pulled, the more the collar would press against his throat. To harness his real power, I needed just that—a harness—but his was hanging on a hook on the inside of my kitchen door.

My sore ribs reminded me of Kaiser's rope. Was it tied to a tree? I had no knife. I retrieved the flashlight from the blacktop by the garage doors, hauled Rowdy across the lawn, and nearly tripped on the rope a second time. I picked it up, pulled in both directions, and began gathering it up. At the dog's end was a metal snap. The other end was tied not to a tree, but to a sturdy metal tethering device, a corkscrew stake. I unscrewed it from the wet earth, and Rowdy and I headed back to the light.

The end of the rope fastened to the corkscrew stake had to go around the door handle; otherwise its sharp spiral could injure Rowdy. The harness I fashioned for him from the snap end of the rope was nothing to brag about. A good harness is made of webbing, not rope. It's padded. Mine wasn't. It's designed for its purpose: It's an X-back sledding harness, a racing harness, a trail harness, or a freight and weight-pull harness. My aim was to approximate any harness at all, and the result was rough in design and rough on Rowdy's breastbone, withers, and forelegs, I'm afraid, but if it worked at all, he'd feel those ropes cutting into his flesh for only a few seconds before the garage door yielded. Or the handle tumbled to the ground. Or the old, wet rope broke. Even when new, it had been more like clothesline than like any rock climber's special, and the combination of Kaiser's lunging and exposure to the elements had obviously weakened it. It was knotted in a couple of places and, in others, beginning to fray.

I knotted the corkscrew-stake end around the sturdier-looking of the garage-door handles, and at the opposite end of the rope, about fifteen feet from the door, positioned my rope-trussed Rowdy to face away from the garage. I got behind him and gripped the slimy rope in both hands. I wouldn't be much help, but I intended to do my share.

The rain was still drifting down in a fine mist, but the thunder and lightning had stopped, and the wind had entirely abated. Ahead of me, Rowdy's wet coat reflected the weak floodlight. Drenched and shed out, he was a bony, ragged creature who looked more like an unkempt wolf than like a malamute. Rain had transformed the plumy white of his tail to limp clumps and spikes. Mud coated his feet and clung to his legs and belly. My hope rested on this skinny gray dog.

"Rowdy, pull!" I shouted suddenly, before I lost my nerve. "Pull!" My voice sounded weak.

When he moved forward, the rope dug and bit into my palms, but the door didn't give.

"Whoa," I said.

I breathed out, and Rowdy stopped. He shook himself off and spattered me with water and mud. The heaviest weight he'd ever pulled before was a light sled with smooth, fast runners designed to glide across snow. He'd never been harnessed to a dead weight, never been asked to haul a loaded sledge, never been told to strain. And he'd never known failure. Until now. But the rope hadn't broken. I renewed my grip on it.

The words that I whispered to Rowdy were the words Jack London gave to Thornton, the words Thornton whispered to the great dog Buck. "As you love me," I whispered. I raised my voice, repeated the words, and added my own: "As you love me. As I love you, Rowdy." Then I shouted: *"PULL! ROWDY, PULL! PULL, BOY! PULL!"*

Head lowered, forelegs bent, crouching as if to flatten himself to the ground, Rowdy gave a single mighty lunge that shot the rope through my hands and burned off skin. His great hind legs struggled, his massive forelegs reached, every muscle of his body drove indomitably forward.

The handle and the frayed rope held, and so did my dog, heaving and straining. With a sudden crack, the big door gave. I had to stop Rowdy before he yanked it from its hinges. What I'd asked him to do had been beyond his strength, and he'd done it, anyway. His muscles didn't force open that door. What did it was sheer will, the will to pull. It's called heart, you know. Great heart. I sank to the wet blacktop and tried to cradle him in my arms, but he just licked my face and wagged his tail. Born to pull.

With Rowdy roped to the door and nothing to use as a knife, I entered the dark garage. The angry male voices still rumbled not far away. I snapped on the flashlight. Ahead was a door. God help me if this is locked, too, I thought, but the knob turned easily in my sore, torn hand. I turned around and ran the beam over Mitch, Jr.'s, Corvette, a big lime-green station wagon, a battered lawn mower, a new snowblower, and a collection of rusty garden tools, including a pair of hand-held grass shears. Back outside, I used their dull blades to saw Rowdy loose from that makeshift harness. When I'd freed him, I called him to heel and returned to the garage, to that unlocked door. I eased it open a crack and held still. Rowdy sat silently at my side. I peered in and listened.

The basement room must have been renovated in the fifties. Some long-ago do-it-yourselfer had stuck acoustic-tile squares on the ceiling and installed recessed lights. The tiles were water-stained. Some of the light fixtures dangled loose. The walls and a flight of stairs directly ahead of me, at the far end of the room, were roughly finished in cheap knotty-pine paneling. The furniture, all painted a loud, hideous orange, consisted of some banged-up kitchen chairs and a great many low tables that looked like discards from an unsavory cocktail lounge. The room also held a long, lumpy-looking couch and two matching chairs, all upholstered in some disgusting, furry black stuff that looked like home-dyed, overprocessed human hair.

Leah sat upright and immobile in the middle of the couch. Her arms were folded across her chest. So far as I could tell, she was unhurt. I couldn't see Kimi. Willie Johnson had one of the human-hair chairs, and the eldest brother, the Corvette-driving, would-be suave Mitch, faced Willie from one of the orange kitchen chairs. Dale was pacing back and forth taking swigs from a can of Miller Light. One of his hands held the beer can. In the other was a black cylinder. He was shouting at his brothers, who were both shouting back at him.

Of the three louts, Mitch had the most penetrating voice and the clearest articulation. I caught his gist pretty quickly.

"One goddamned stupid mistake of yours after another," he hollered, jabbing a finger toward Dale. The jacket of a dark suit hung over the back of his chair, his white shirt was sweat-stained, and he'd undone the knot of his red power tie. "Every damned thing you've ever done you've screwed up. And then when you screw it up, and somebody comes in and tries to un-screw it for you, do you help? Hell, no. No, not you. You don't need anybody's help, do you? Well, this time, I've had it. Let your loudmouth friends get you out of this one." He leaned back and fiddled with his tie.

Dale crumbled his beer can in his fist, threw it against the wall, and bellowed what I took to be a defense of his loudmouth friends. After Mitch, Jr., had given him a reply that was mostly about his Corvette, his college degree, and the upward path that stretched before him in spite of Dale's efforts to drag him and the rest of the family down, the two of them started in on their father.

"So go wake the old man," Mitch sneered. He stood up and immediately sat down.

"Screw you, Mitch," Dale said drunkenly. "Right. Go and suck up to the old man. And cut the crap about you always try-ing to help me, Mitch. In our whole life you never stood up for me once, not one time, not when I was a little kid, even. You remember Buddy, Mitch? You remember Buddy?" He stomped toward Mitch and loomed over him. His face and voice shared a raw, stupid intensity. "You stood up for me real good then, didn't you?" I expected him to start sobbing, but instead of cry-ing, he staggered across the room and tore another can of Miller Light from a six-pack that sat on top of two others on one of the orange tables. He popped open the can and upended it over his open mouth. He looked like an albino black Angus bottle-feeding itself.

"Hey, Dale, lay off that," said Mitch, wiping sweat off his neck.

"Screw you, Mitch," Dale mumbled.

"There are things you gotta do, little brother," said Mitch.

"Always things I gotta do, right? I always gotta do them. Ever since Buddy, right? I'm always the one's gotta do everything, right, Mitch?" He lurched back across the room and stared at Mitch. "'Cause everything's always my fault around here, right?"

Buddy? Some kid they'd grown up with? A fourth brother? If so, wouldn't he have appeared on Edna's family tree? I of all people should have guessed.

"Dale," Mitch said soberly, pulling his neck up high and straight, "I hate to be the one to break you the news, but Buddy would've ended up just like Kaiser, anyways."

So far, Willie had kept himself pretty much out of the fight except to nod and grunt occasional support for Mitch. Mostly, he'd been keeping an eye on Leah, whose body looked frozen and whose gaze was fixed ahead of her. But now he changed sides.

"Mitch, shut up," he said. "It wasn't Dale that was mean to Buddy. It was you."

"Yeah," said Dale, staggering to Willie and thumping him on the back. "And Mom and Dad didn't do a goddamned thing but lay it all on me like always." He sounded about eight years old. Then, to my amazement, he backed up a step and began shouting at Willie. "Yeah and after Buddy, and after they scream and yell if Kaiser sticks his nose in the house, she lets goddamned Righteous eat in the kitchen and sleep right in your bed, and does she give you that shit about fleas? Hell, no! Oh, no, 'cause it's real different. It's precious little Willie's dog, right?"

"Right," Mitch said. "Nothing's ever your fault, is it, Dale?"

"Goddamn well not my fault," agreed Dale, who seemed genuinely to have missed the point. "For Christ's sake, Mitch! I was only a kid."

"Dale, this isn't Buddy we're talking about," Mitch insisted. "Buddy's history."

"Come on, Dale," Willie added. "He's right. We been over that a million times."

"Well, screw you!" Dale shouted. "Screw both you! Buddy'd still be alive, you know! He'd be old, but he'd still be alive! Screw both of you! He'd still be alive!"

"Yeah, and so would the Jew next door," said Mitch.

"That was an accident, and you know it," Dale yelled, as if Rose's death had been a puddle left on the floor by a puppy he'd forgotten to walk. "And it was all her own goddamned fault. I mean, it's my dog, right? It's *my* dog. It was none of her goddamned business. You know what she was trying to do? She was trying to take my dog away. If she'd kept her big Jew nose out of it, none of it would've happened."

Why are so many gentiles timid about saying *Jew*? Because we've heard slime like Dale Johnson cough it up and spit it out the way he did, and that's the truth.

But it didn't bother Mitch. "Dale, when you do something that might or might not kill somebody, and it does, then it's not an accident."

"And if you'd kept your nose out of my business," Willie added coldly, "we wouldn't be in *this* mess."

"Oh, yeah? Well, lemme tell you what this little bitch thought, baby brother," said Dale, glaring at Leah. "She thought you weren't good enough for her." He huffed himself up and added, "Nobody treats my little brother like that, going out with a goddamned Jew and treating my little brother like shit." He grabbed a can of beer, opened it, downed it, and reached for another.

"Dale, that's enough," Mitch ordered him. "There are things we gotta do. You gotta get out of here."

"Well, screw you, you bastard! You get outta here!" Dale shouted. Finding himself near a wall, he leaned on it.

Mitch and Willie seemed to study one another. I expected them to come up with some plan that they'd try to sell to Dale, but they didn't. Instead, Mitch turned on Willie and began laying blame on him, and Willie tried to defend himself.

"If you'd kept your goddamned mouth shut," Mitch was yelling at Willie, but Willie interrupted him.

"If I'd kept my so-called goddamned mouth shut," said Willie, "her and her aunt would've gone and got him locked up, and not just about Kaiser, either, Mitch. I had to tell him, Mitch, honest to God, like I told you, the aunt knows about Mrs. Engleman. I heard her tonight. She was asking about shock collars. And I heard Leah saying she got the pictures. Mitch, I had to tell him."

"Shit," Dale said, "I'm not afraid of them. I already got them good." He laughed and waved the black cylinder around.

"Dale," Mitch lectured him, "so her goddamned aunt's got the pictures. What good's that gonna do you?"

"Yeah, Dale," Willie added. "Nobody cares about the dog now. Dale, will you listen? I told you, she was asking about shock collars, and if you turn yourself in, all's it is is manslaughter. But you gotta do it. You gotta get that it's serious. Nobody cares about the dog anymore."

"Yeah," Dale shouted painfully, "'cause it's only *my* dog."

"Jesus, Willie," Mitch said. "Would you lay off dogs?"

"Yeah, lay off," Dale said. "Goddamned well leave my dogs the hell alone. They're my goddamned dogs, and nobody's taking my goddamned dogs away from me."

"So take your goddamned dog with you," Mitch said. "Nobody's gonna miss him. Just get the hell out of here, and I'll take care of the rest." The rest. Leah. Kimi. "Dale, you gotta really get it. It's over. It's too late."

Mitch should have known better than to make any sudden moves, but he rose abruptly, took a couple of long strides toward Dale, and tried to snatch the black cylinder from Dale's hand. Dale, though, was brawnier than Mitch and quicker than Mitch had anticipated. When he sidestepped, Mitch crashed into one of the coffee tables. Dale began laughing and waving the black cylinder around, then suddenly held it still and pointed it toward a corner of the room, a corner that was out of my view. His eyes brightened, and crazy as this may sound, his face softened in simple happiness. He pressed the button.

Kimi's yelps of pain rang in my ears. Leah began screaming and screaming. Rowdy, who'd been sitting still and keeping absolutely quiet, suddenly barged ahead of me, shoved open the door, and hurled himself into the room. Unsure of his intentions and my own, I followed. What happened next was, I think, the weirdest event in the whole nightmare.

From the top of the flight of stairs came Edna's voice. "Boys?" she called almost sweetly. "Boys? What's going on down there?" She sounded like a den mother who'd caught her little scouts in the middle of a major pillow fight.

The effect was sudden. All three of her sons held still and stayed quiet. Dale must have taken his finger off the button on the transmitter, because Kimi stopped yelping. Then, as if prompted by someone offstage, Mitch, Dale, and Willie all began laughing.

"It's nothing, Mom," Mitch called. "Go to bed."

"Well, if you boys don't settle down," she scolded, "you're going to wake up your father."

"Relax, Mom," Dale called to her. "We've just caught a burglar is all. We've just caught a burglar!"

At the top of the stairs, a door clicked shut.

I'd used the distraction Edna offered to grab Rowdy's collar and pull him with me toward Kimi. Miss Malamute Power, who'd never once before seemed even slightly disconcerted by anything whatsoever, was shaking. Around her neck was a thick collar encased in heavy black electrician's tape. The shock collars—oh, pardon me, electronic trainers—I'd seen before in the catalogs and ads hadn't looked anything like this one. It was much thicker than any collar I'd ever seen before, heavy all the way around, and I was having trouble finding a buckle. Had he taped the collar on? My fingers groped, searching for a loose piece, something to pull. Before I found anything, Dale noticed me.

He stared blearily at me, held up the transmitter, and grinned. He didn't say anything. He didn't need to. I sat on the floor next to Kimi, lifted one hand rapidly upward in front of Rowdy's nose to tell him to lie down, and then put a hand on each of my dogs. I slid the hand that rested on Kimi slowly under the tight, tight collar and felt for the plugs. There were two. I squeezed my fingers between those plugs and Kimi's neck. I held still, waiting.

Chapter 28

DALE Johnson should have known better than to tease Edna about a burglar, and his brothers should have known better than to let him get away with it. All three should have realized that their mother had no sense of humor.

The only person facing the stairs, I saw her before the others knew she'd come back. Edna, my savior, descended very quietly. Her feet appeared first. She wore grubby green terry-cloth slippers. Her calves were scrawny. A couple of inches of black lace nightie—black lace, you never can tell—dangled below a mustard-colored rayon robe. A flesh-toned hairnet covered most of her head. She was carrying a shotgun. I was sure it was a Browning, and I thought it was an A-500 like my father's. He bought it because he has a streak of vanity, I suppose—the A-500 is one of the Buck Specials.

Edna's sons didn't hear her because they'd resumed their quarrel. Mitch was arguing with both of the others and yelling at me to stay put. Mitch claimed that if Dale took off and disappeared for a while, everything could be handled, or so he told his brothers. None of them noticed Edna until she'd almost reached the bottom step. I'm not sure whether Willie or Mitch saw her first, but it was Dale, the closest to her and the one on his feet, who acted.

"Jesus Christ," he said gently. "Mom, gimme that. Hey, I was only kidding. There's no burglar. Mom, gimme that."

He put his beer can and the transmitter on one of the tables, reached out, and took the Buck Special from her. She didn't resist. Then she stood there with her arms hanging helplessly at her sides. She looked bewildered, but no more than the last time I'd seen her.

183

Either the feel of the Browning or his mother's presence,
maybe both, renewed Dale's energy. He started telling his
brothers that he wasn't going anywhere. Then he launched into
a jumble of inarticulate, pained accusations. Most were about
Buddy. None were directed to Edna, who was gazing around
with mean, empty eyes. Dale was well into his tirade when a
man I'd never seen before wove his way down the stairs. I didn't
know him, but the close atmosphere of the damp cellar reeked
of his invisible companion, a guy named Jim Beam.

Although the father and his sons all resembled one another,
Mitchell Dale Johnson, Sr., looked most like an aged, wasted
version of Dale. He had the same big-boned, wide build, but
without the flesh and youth. His vague, bloodshot eyes said he
was as drunk as Dale, too. His face and neck were a sickly, wrinkled yellow-gray. Gray-blond hair stood out from his head in
strange waves, like the gelled and crimped coiffure of a very old
woman. In freakish contrast to Edna and to his own disheveled
drunkenness, though, he was fastidiously and expensively
dressed in a red plaid Pendleton robe over white linen pajamas.
His black leather bedroom slippers gleamed. He even wore
socks.

He was evidently just sober enough to have caught the gist
of Dale's rambling. "Shut your drunken trap about Buddy," he
ordered Dale. He slurred his words less than I'd expected.
"Buddy was a useless piece of shit, like that goddamned thing
you've got now. I shouldn't've bothered to get him gassed. I
should've wrung his neck myself."

Dale turned slowly toward his father. His face had lost the
pleasure I'd seen when he'd been waving the transmitter
around. In fact, the expression on his thick, lifeless features was
completely flat; he didn't have one. He calmly raised the shotgun, squeezed the trigger, and shot his father dead. With a Buck
Special at a range of about three yards, the second shot was a
little superfluous, but Dale evidently didn't want to take any
chances.

Both blasts filled my ears with what felt like burning paraffin.
The odor of blood and gun blended sickeningly with the reek
of beer and Jim Beam. Most of what had been Mitchell Dale
Johnson, Sr., was distributed in red, gray, and white spatters
over the cellar stairs. I'm not squeamish, but I wish I hadn't

seen his feet. They still wore socks and those black leather slippers.

Still carrying the gun, Dale finally took Mitch's advice. He stalked out through the door to the garage. Seconds later, an engine started, and Mitch, who'd been trying to make Edna stop screaming, tore for the door in a rage. "That's my Corvette!" he yelled. "He's stealing my Corvette!"

I took advantage of the chaos. With Rowdy's lead in one sore hand and that deadly collar in the other, I stood up and nodded to Leah to follow me. As the four of us stumbled out to the garage, no one tried to stop us. Willie had taken over Edna, and he must have heard the sirens, anyway, and known it was over.

When we got outside, two police cruisers blocked the street, and a third, doors open, headlights glaring, idled about halfway down the driveway. Mitch was standing at the bottom of the drive staring at the shattered windshield of his Corvette, which had never even reached the street. One cop was holding the Browning, and another two kept Dale upright between them. His hands were in cuffs. There was blood on his face, and he was screaming at the cops: "I'm bleeding! Look what you did! I'm bleeding! You bastards shot me! You shot *me*!"

What choice did they have? Dale had been aiming the Buck Special directly at them. They had to defend themselves. The bullet had nicked his ear.

Chapter 29

"Ever," Rita emphasized. "This was a family in which no one could *ever* leave home. That was one meaning of Mother's symptom."

"Would you not call her Mother?" I said. "Her name is Edna."

"Sorry," Rita said. "It's kind of a professional tic."

Dale had been in custody for two days. Leah was at the Newton-Wellesley Hospital visiting Jeff, and Rita and I were sharing a dinner of take-out Chinese food in her kitchen.

"Anyway," she went on, "the agoraphobia was like a family banner she carried, a cross, if you will, and it was a heavy one. She made a big sacrifice to make sure everyone got the message: Don't leave home. Her role was to act that rule out, to make it highly explicit. And, of course, the others supported her in it. They made it possible for her to make that contribution to the family."

"Doing the shopping."

"And everything else. And when the others leave home, go to work, where do they go?"

"Home away from home. The family business. And the names, right? I mean, how many families are there where three people all have the same name?"

"In itself," Rita said, "it isn't necessarily pathological, but in this context?"

"Rita, you want to know the weirdest thing? After everything Dale did, it's weird, but I feel sorry for him, because of Buddy. That's what started it. You know, Jack Engleman knew about that? So did Rose. The incredible thing is that the dog, Buddy, was supposed to be therapy for him. When Dale was whatever,

seven or eight, he was already in trouble, and some counselor
at school talked the parents into buying him a dog. As therapy,
right? He was bullying the other kids around and getting in
fights and stuff. And the dog was supposed to socialize him."

"Only nobody looked at the family," Rita said.

"Right. So these monsters get him the dog, but what do they
do? They make him promise that he has to take total care of
it. He's a little kid, right? And he's supposed to be a hundred
percent responsible. So, naturally, he isn't. He can't be. He's too
young, and he's a screwed up kid, anyway. So his doting parents
decide that here's the chance to give him a good lesson in re-
sponsibility, keeping his promises, all that. I heard this from
Willie and Mitch, that night. Anyway, the parents take the dog
to some shelter, and then they come home and tell Dale all
about Buddy being gassed to death, and they actually tell him
that it's his punishment, because he didn't keep his promise. Is
that unbelievable?"

"No," Rita said sadly.

"You mean you . . . ?"

"In my business, you've heard everything before," Rita said.

"When he talked about Buddy, honest to God, Rita, it was
the only time he was real, in a way. The rest of the time, he
was yelling and storming around and everything, but it felt hollow, I guess. And when he aimed at his father? And even when
he shot him? His face was totally empty. Blank. He could've
been aiming the remote control at a VCR. Except he definitely
liked aiming that remote trainer at Kimi. He liked causing pain,
all right."

"Giving what he got," Rita said.

"But when he talked about Buddy, there was real pain. You
could hear it in his voice. He was like a little kid. It was as if
it'd just happened."

"For him, it had," Rita said. "That's the point. It was always
still happening, over and over again. Everyone was someone
taking his dog away. Rose Engleman? And Leah? And you?
You were all the same person, gassing his dog."

"That's the other thing," I said. "About the gas. His parents
actually told him all about the gas chambers at the shelter or
wherever it was. Shelter, right. And somehow he got it hooked
up with the . . . the holocaust. I heard that from Kevin. I mean,
the family were all anti-Semites, but apparently Dale—not

when he was a little kid, but later—when he heard about the concentration camps and everything, he got sort of obsessed. But wouldn't you think he'd have taken the side of the victims?"

Rita shook her head. "Identification with the aggressor, it's called," she said. "The ones who did the gassing. The ones in control. The ones who cause pain. So he's one of them. It's the oldest story in the world, really. The abused become the abusers."

"Well, he got his revenge," I said. "I guess the miracle is that he didn't shoot Edna, too. Anyway, about Leah?"

"She's relieved that Jeff's okay. She's very angry at Willie, of course. She feels betrayed. She doesn't understand that the nature of that family was such that he *had* to tell Dale. In that family, the alliances were just as strong as the antagonisms. They were so enmeshed that a threat to one of them was a personal threat to everyone. So when Willie heard you asking about shock collars, and then he heard Leah say something about having the pictures, he put it together and went home to tell Dale. Only, of course, instead of taking off or turning himself in, Dale found out where Leah was. Willie was in that class with Leah and Jeff, and he was there when they left. And I'm sure Dale had no trouble getting that out of him, and Willie knew where Jeff lived. It's right on that list from your dog club. So all Dale had to do was wait at Jeff's. Then he followed them."

"If I'd listened to Steve, I'd've—"

"Speaking of whom," Rita interrupted.

"Yeah. It's okay now," I said. "But it did take him an awfully long time to get the police to the Johnsons', although it wasn't as long as it seemed then. But they wasted a whole lot of time in the woods."

"Holly, if you didn't know where you were going, how was Steve supposed to know where you were?"

"Because he's a vet," I said, "which means he's supposed to know everything. It's one of the burdens of high priesthood. Anyway, he was right, about stopping at the woods, even though he was wrong about whose idea it was. It was Leah's, and it never occurred to me, because I thought, well, she knows they can come here! And I knew about the Eliot Woods. I'm even the one who told Steve it was a lovers' lane. It never crossed my mind that they'd be so stupid. You know, they weren't even in the car when he smashed the window? He was after the pictures, and I guess that's where he thought they'd be. And Kimi was with them, not that she would've tried to protect the car or anything. And she might've done something when he attacked Jeff, but when Jeff went to see what was going on, he made Leah keep Kimi with her. And after that, there was nothing Leah could do, because he slapped that collar on Kimi, so all she did was try to spare Kimi."

"Speaking of which," Rita said, "she must've got some jolt. Is she all right?"

"Yeah, I think so. Malamutes are tough, and she's tough even for a malamute. She probably wouldn't want to walk into that cellar again, but obviously she won't have to. The dogs' ears are probably still ringing—mine are—but I think their hearing is okay."

"So, look," Rita said. "There's one other thing. Did he actually plan to kill Rose? How could he have known . . . ?"

"Did he know about the pacemaker? Probably not. But one thing he did know about was electricity, because, it turns out, he took electronics in high school. When I thought about who'd know about electricity, mostly I thought about Dr. Zager, you know, drills and stuff. And it never occurred to me that if he got off on beating the dog, he'd really, really get off on a shock collar. I didn't put it together until I saw the deer rifle."

Rita looked puzzled.

"Hunters," I explained. "Really, obedience people don't use those things that much. Hunters do. They're the big market for shock collars. I should've known. Right on their coffee table, they had *Outdoor Life,* for God's sake. Anyway, I've thought a lot about whether he planned to kill her. One thing is, I don't see how he could've known about the pacemaker. But, on the other hand, one thing he'd've learned about in school is electrical safety. And hazards. So he'd know about water, that it's a great conductor, and he'd know that some people can survive gigantic shocks, and that sometimes, a really small shock, like fifty volts, can kill you. In a way, that's the worst of it."

"What is?"

"That he didn't know. I don't think anyone's going to end up proving it, but if you ask me, he didn't know whether she'd just get a bad shock or whether it'd kill her. He thought he'd killed Jeff. If you'd seen Jeff, you'd see why. I thought he'd killed him, too. But with Rose, if you ask me, he just didn't care. Probably if she'd lived, he'd have threatened to do the same thing to Caprice unless she gave him the pictures and kept her mouth shut. But he didn't care one way or the other about whether she lived or died. After what his parents did to him? After Buddy? Rita, when they killed his dog, they half killed him. How was he supposed to know the difference?"

Chapter 30

MITCHELL Dale Johnson, Jr., you'll recall, having calmly watched his brother Dale shoot their father, lost his temper only when he realized that Dale was stealing his Corvette. After that noble demonstration of his firm sense of priorities, Mitch was awarded the guardianship of his mother, Edna, but I suppose that the court didn't have much choice. Dale would hardly have been suitable, and Willie was a bit young for the task. At any rate, Mitch rather quickly sold the house next to Jack Engleman's and took advantage of the depressed market to buy a three-bedroom condo near Kendall Square in Cambridge. One of the extra bedrooms is for Edna, who is supposed to move in with Mitch as soon as she's discharged from the psychiatric hospital. The other bedroom is not, as you might suppose, for Willie, but for Dale, in case he gets a furlough or an early release, I guess. Willie, you see, has broken the family rule. He's been accepted at a junior college with a canine science program. He'll spend two years learning to groom and handle dogs. I wonder whether he'll come home for Christmas.

Speaking of Christmas, I never wrote that article about Marcia Brawley, but she finished the scarf for Buck, and I paid her for it. It's still here, packed in mothballs. I'll have to decide whether to give it to him. If I do, I won't tell him what else she puts around people's necks . . . or, more precisely, around dogs' necks.

Dr. Charlotte Zager's fluoride treatments have done wonders for my teeth, and contrary to Buck's predictions, haven't affected my politics at all. Her son moved into his new offices, and when Steve told Rita that there was nothing more he could do for Groucho, she started taking Groucho to Dr. Don Zager for acupuncture treatments. Groucho is as stiff and lame as ever, and his yellow-tinged eyes stare more and more deeply into no-where, but Rita is convinced that his energy is improving, and she likes Dr. Zager a lot. In fact, she and Don Zager have had dinner together twice, but I am not optimistic about their future. Some interfaith relationships work fine, but theirs is a doomed combination: She is devout Cambridge, and he's born-again California.

Jim O'Brian adopted Tina's rescue dog, the malamute bitch. He named her Rose. It seemed a peculiar choice to me, but Jack didn't mind. He told me that it's a Jewish custom not to name your children after the living and that Rose would've been flat-tered.

In late August, Kimi completed her C.D. in three straight trials and with good scores, too. Leah handled her. Not long afterward, on the morning Leah left, the phone rang about two dozen times. Not one of the calls was for me. Leah went out to visit Kevin Dennehy's mother and a lot of other neighbors. After that, Miriam, Ian, Seth, and some more people came over to say good-bye to her. They played a lot of loud music. Miriam somehow ended up wearing a sweatshirt that I recognized as mine, but I didn't say anything about it. Jeff brought a single red rose, and I dragged the dogs away so he and Leah could have some time alone in the living room.

Rowdy and Kimi, of course, knew that she was leaving. Even the stupidest obedience-school flunk-out knows when someone's going away, but the ancestral memory of Alaskan malamutes reminds them that no one hangs around on a fast-disintegrating ice floe to whistle for a stray pup. Eyes bright, muscles tense, ears pricked up, new fall coats gleaming, they sniffed Leah's luggage, barricaded the door, pranced from room to room, and tried their best to look too cute to leave behind.

When Leah and Jeff finally emerged, they were both crying so contagiously that I started in, too, and hugged them both. The dogs, of course, barged in, and all of us clung to Leah as if we'd never hear from her again. Then I drove her to the air-port, where we met Arthur and Cassie's plane. I hated to turn her over to them. I tried to remember that it was for only one more year.

When I got home, the house was weirdly quiet. Miriam had left my sweatshirt, and no one had borrowed anything else. The phone didn't ring. I vacuumed. I scrubbed the bathroom. No one undid my work. The dogs kept nosing around.

"Don't look at me," I told them. "I didn't throw her out. She had to leave. She had to go home."

Then the three of us went to Leah's empty room. I sat on her bed and patted the mattress to tell Rowdy and Kimi that it was okay for them to join me. They did. I wasn't really alone. No one with two Alaskan malamutes is ever alone. Or lonely. It's just that we felt that way.

Cassie sent me a perfunctory thank-you letter, and over the next few months, Leah called now and then, mostly to ask about the dogs. I made Rowdy and Kimi woo-woo into the phone and kept her up-to-date on their training. She said she was busy studying, taking all those tests, and doing her college applications.

Then one day in November, the phone rang. At first, I didn't recognize Arthur's voice. I thought I'd got an obscene phone call.

"You have completely blown her chances! Do you realize that?" The voice was enraged.

"Arthur?" I asked incredulously.

"I knew it was all a terrible mistake. I knew it, I knew it. The plane fare would've been cheap at this price. Her whole life! It's her whole life she's ruining!"

"Arthur, slow down. Sit down. Take a deep breath, and then blow it out."

"Blow it out! Blow it out!"

"Arthur, this is Holly Winter," I said. "Cassie's niece? Maybe you dialed my number by mistake."

He may actually have taken my advice about the deep breath, but the ensuing exhalation was no act of wordless, mind-clearing stress reduction. If he gasped in a lungful of air, all he did was spend a few seconds oxygenating his fury before he propelled it out, over the phone wires, and into my innocent left ear. Three words were clear: *Leah, Harvard,* and *dogs.* Then he started to groan and cry. During Leah's stay with me, I had, of course, begun to reconsider and reevaluate my parents' view of Arthur. Could such a mental and moral weakling have sired Leah? But this pathetic ranting made me realize that my parents may have been right, after all. The maternal stock must have been prepotent; Arthur's get showed the traits of her mother's line, none of Arthur's.

Cassie finally got on the phone. Her distress equaled Arthur's, it seemed to me, but she held herself together enough to inform me of its cause. Until today, Leah had seemed to her parents to be submissively following the family plan of completing a successful application to that place down the street from my house. I should add that Leah was, in fact, complying with the application requirements. She had not only taken but had excelled on numerous acronymic tests of language and mathematical ability and other tests of achievement in English, math, chemistry, and, of all things, Latin. Her grades were high, her recommendations sensational, her extracurricular activities diverse. In other words, she was such a perfect specimen of the breed, virtually the standard incarnate, that the judges were sure to put her up. Or so it had seemed. Until now. And it was all my fault.

Gaining admission to Harvard, it seems, is not exactly like getting a place in the ribbons at a dog show. In the breed ring, the dog has to trot around, hold a pose, and look happy while a stranger stares and pokes; and in obedience, he has to demonstrate a mastery of the exercises and complete attention to the commands of the handler. But to win? In either ring, he also has to show off, strut his stuff, hold his head up, put some energy into his step, and announce to the judge that he's the obvious, unmistakable number one. Leah, it seemed to me, had done all of that, but, as I've said, there is one surprising difference between the requirements of Harvard and those of the American Kennel Club: Dogs are never expected to speak for themselves. Leah, though, had to submit a series of essays, and, at least in her parents' view, she'd stubbornly and deliberately NQ'd—not qualified—by failing that last exercise.

I knew precisely how they felt. It's happened to me. In Novice and Open, of course, the last exercise is the long down. You get through everything else with a 200, step confidently toward the dog with five seconds to go until that perfect score, and then watch helplessly as he rises to a sit and your heart sinks. He might as well have lagged, forged, sat crooked, failed the recall, and dropped his dumbbell. You might as well never have trained at all. You might as well have stayed home. Or, in Leah's case, she might as well have gone to public kindergarten instead of Montessori, read the complete works of Robert Ludlum instead of Jane Austen, and scored minus 800 on all the tests. Most of all, she should have stayed home. She should have stayed with her parents, not with me. Why is that?

Cassie read me the NQ'ing essay. Her voice sounded nothing like my mother's. I felt sorry for Arthur and Cassie, but I knew that there was no cause for alarm. Leah's statement was succinct and truthful. Why *did* she want to go to Harvard? Well, Harvard *is* located conveniently near the Nonantum and Cambridge dog training clubs. Harvard Square *is* an ideal place to train because, damn it, it really *is* a lot like a dog show. *Veritas,* you know. Truth. That's Harvard's motto.

"So what's the problem?" I asked Cassie. "She's a shoo-in. She'll be back in Cambridge next fall. The dogs will be thrilled."

Cassie hung up.